ROSE IN CHARGE

*In Charlotte —
'Rose' sends
her best!
Barbara Dickson
4/30/18*

A ROSE MCNESS MYSTERY

DORRANCE
PUBLISHING CO
EST. 1920
PITTSBURGH, PENNSYLVANIA 15238

Dorrance Publishing Co
585 Alpha Drive
Pittsburgh, PA 15238
Visit our website at www.dorrancebookstore.com

ISBN: 978-1-4809-5191-4
eISBN: 978-1-4809-5169-3

COVER ART and ILLUSTRATIONS by the author.

WHEN ROSE MCNESS AGREES TO JOIN HER FRIEND, noted lichenologist Dr. Frances Keynes-Livingston in England, little does she imagine the adventures that await. Arriving in London, Rose learns that the duo is headed for the village of East Plumley where someone has been stealing headstones from the centuries-old graveyard of the parish church. With her usual grit and can-do attitude, Rose discovers that there is more happening in this quiet hamlet than meets the eye. As Dr. Keynes-Livingston endeavors to uncover the scientific aspects of the thefts, Rose endears herself to many of the town's characters as she does her own exploring and eavesdropping. The town's premier baker, a pair of handymen, an attractive vicar and a questionable 'alterations lady' present an array of suspects of the crime. Surprises abound as ROSE IN CHARGE completes her journey.

Also by Barbara Dickinson

A Rebellious House
Small House, Large World
Lifeguards and Safeguards
Secrets from My Kitchen
Grandfather Jumper and the Cookie Eating Monsters
(a picture book for children)

Books do not write themselves.

I am deeply and happily indebted to many members of my immediate family and to scores of good friends for their outpouring of love and countless suggestions, all of which helped build a better book. My thanks to Tim Rogers, my son, who named this book years ago when I wasn't even thinking of reviving Rose; to my daughter, Hilary King, who was indispensable with both editing and encouragement; to each member of the Rector's Book Club at St. John's Episcopal Church in Roanoke, Virginia, who were among the first to read *"Rose"* and offered sound nuggets of wisdom that I took to heart and computer; to Tom Noyes and members of the writer's group at Chautauqua, '16; to Helen Vogel, a trusted friend who offered honest criticism and encouragement when "Rose" – and the author – were limping towards the finish line; to Jocey and Marjorie, of Sussex, who counseled in all things British; and last but not least my devoted editor/typist/friend. Nancy McDaniel, who has been with me from the beginning.

I wish I could include hugs to each of you within these pages.

Barbara Dickinson

This one is for Tim.

"It is better to know some of the questions than all of the answers."

James Thurber

Preamble

NOT SO VERY FAR WEST AND SOUTH of the Shenandoah Valley there is a serenity in the rolling acres surrounding the sprawling structure the locals call "old man" Wynfield's folly. The hundred plus residents of Wynfield Farms fondly call it home.

Owned by the Nottingham Corporation for the past decade, the imposing property accrued by railroad magnate Samuel Thomas Wynfield underwent many modifications and revisions to become the place it is now. Providential wisdom led the Corporation's 'powers that be' to leave much of the precious acreage untouched.

Despite, or perhaps because of, structural additions to the original manse, its stone facade holds a mellow patina that belies its age. Casement windows reflect the evening's western glow. Gardeners monitor pesky tendrils of ivy that jeopardize precarious masonry. Tall chimneys (the promotional brochure counts fourteen) send plumes of smoke upward on the chilliest of mornings, when residents prefer to gather close to the immense, wood burning fireplaces located in all the common rooms. Cards, conversation and, more often than not, a wee dram or two before dinner bring the residents ever closer.

At night, stars wink in a blue-black sky, veiling Wynfield's rounded hills and lush secluded hollows. Deer graze on grasses wet with dew and a waning moon plays tag with slivers of shadows. Sleek-coated chipmunks and voles scurry to nibble the groundcover's tiny berries, while an armada of rabbits darts through thickets of new clover. Breezes sift through boughs of dancing evergreen and infuse the air with the pungent tang of pine and cedar. Many miles away, rushing cars echo highway bedlam. In this valley, on the cusp of a new dawn, only the breathing of night creatures can be heard. There is no hint of mystery at Wynfield Farms—only a resident seeking answers to one.

Chapter One

Rose McNess sighed and stretched her legs as far as the covers allowed. *How did I get tangled up in these blankets? Umm. Bit of sun. Maybe there's a hint of spring coming to Wynfield Farms. Or at least a preview.*

"First things first: coffee. Oh, drat, is that my phone? It *is*. Where is the darn thing? Wait a minute, wait a minute, I'm . . . here it is. Hello? Who? Amaryllis? Amaryllis? Oh, for heaven's sake: where are you? Wait a sec, you're going too fast for these old ears. Where? London? Not Australia? Left? Permanently? Oh, sweetie: I'm so sorry. You did love him so. You're what? Me? No, Amaryllis, I … no, you've got the wrong person. Well, yes, of course I love the British Isles. Yes, I know Browning's 'Oh to be in England.' Oh, stop it, Amaryllis, what sort of mysterious caper are you talking about? Well, maybe . . . you did WHAT? How did you know I would agree to such a thing? I hope you don't want this to be kept secret. Everyone here practically stands and salutes when a registered letter arrives. Yes, yes, I will get myself ready. As ready as any old lady can get ready. All right darling, it's glorious to hear your voice . . . even with such a proposition. On to Heathrow! My word! Now I really need that coffee."

Rose McNess, 79 years of age, twice widowed, ten-year resident of Wynfield Farms, walked purposefully and steadily through her small condominium into the even smaller kitchen and punched the ON button of her percolator. As she waited for that first cup of aromatic black liquid to appear, she sank into the worn maple rocker by the window. The spectacular view from her south window had convinced her to move to this retirement home and to this specific condominium. The Blue Ridge Mountains rose above acres of rolling farmland, farmland that bordered exquisite gardens landscaped with boxwoods and indigenous flora and fauna specifically chosen for the Wynfield acreage.

I came here literally kicking and screaming, but how I do love this place. And my view! This is home, truly home. And now Amaryllis has persuaded me to leave. Whoa, I must not be thinking straight: have I lost the one rational piece of mind that I have . . . or HAD? Amaryllis, how could you do this to me? Rose, how could you agree to such a thing? Amaryllis sending me, registered mail if you please, first class roundtrip tickets to London, leaving next Monday. Next Monday! Which gives me exactly four days to get ready.

Golly, sure glad my passport is current. What sort of mystery is she getting us into? Yes, US, as I've agreed to be her accomplice.

Oh, this coffee is restoring some of my senses. I must call Annie: she'll know what to do. Daughters always do.

ॐ

"Annie? Are you awake?"

"Mother? Are you all right? Have you fallen?"

"No, no, darling, I'm fine. I just—"

"But its six-thirty in the morning: why are you up so early?"

"Darling Annie, I'm fine. Really. But sit down and let me tell you about the phone call I've just had."

"You've won the lottery again."

"Oh, I wish. Even better: I'm going to England."

"Mother: are you serious? You've never mentioned—"

"If you listen, dear, I'll explain. My old friend, Amaryllis, *aka* Frances Keynes-Livingston, just called from London. She's convinced me to help her study something in a small English village, and further convinced me by sending me round-trip tickets to London."

"Must be an English village full of lichen. Isn't she the one who traipsed all over Wynfield Farms in her pith helmet and boots, collecting lichen and bugs?"

"That's Amaryllis! You may not know that she got her doctorate in lichenology. From Harvard, no less. Not many of her ilk around. I'm guessing that this has something to do with her specialty."

Annie laughed. "There aren't many of Amaryllis' *ilk* anywhere! Pith helmet, khakis, boots. Then the next minute grey silk and heels, looking for a bridge partner. Do I remember her! But I also recall that she was very, well, starchy, imperious. *Not* easy. Were you and she very close when she lived at Wynfield, Mom?"

Rose chuckled. "We were, Annie. Amaryllis is really a kind person. Reserved, private, but *kind*. It's the 'Main Line' starch that accounts for her, shall I say, 'outward appearance.' I was always in awe of her, particularly after she did such a bang-up job as chairman of our first talent night. When she came out playing her accordion . . . with her pearls looped around her neck. Do you remember her pearls, dear?"

"Do I ever! Big as marbles and obviously real. But back to the trip. Are you sure you want to tackle this, Mom? Why would you want to travel with 'aloof Amaryllis'? I mean, this could be a lot of work for you. Even dangerous. Really, why knock yourself out when you could sign up for a leisurely tour of England?"

"I've just told Amaryllis yes. I must go. And, I admit, I'm getting rather excited now that I've had a chance to think it over. It just may be the last great adventure I'll ever have! I'm *not* getting any younger you know, in case you haven't noticed. Solving a mystery in some little English village. Golly! Don't you think that sounds exciting, Annie?"

"Oh, Mom, detectives don't go around saying 'golly'!"

"Don't be so negative. You know I just say' golly' when I get nervous. Or frustrated. It just pops out-without my realizing what I'm saying."

"All right, if you are determined to go, *when* do you leave?"

"Monday morning. *This* coming Monday morning. Could you please call your brothers for me and tell them where I am going? I won't have time to call and explain everything."

"Happy to be of service, and I'll explain all. Not that I know that much. That'll save you a few phone calls. Be sure to pack your long-johns; England can be damp and cold in March."

"You are so right, darling. If I don't talk to you between now and Monday, much love!" Mother and daughter surrendered phones and Rose poured herself more coffee. Family notified thanks to my efficient daughter. I believe it is now time to let a few friends in on my adventure.

"Father Charlie? Awake? It's Rose, here."

"Rose McNess, of course I'm awake and just back from my morning constitutional."

"Do you mean the coffee and doughnuts in the lobby sort, or a *real* constitutional?"

"The former, Rose. I'm a wimp and you know it. What's on your mind this Thursday?"

"I am busting to tell someone about my forthcoming adventure, and since you remember Amaryllis so well—"

"Frances Keynes-Livingston? Of course. I remember her very well. Not the most neighborly of associates but who could forget those pearls, or her winning hands at bridge? She scalped me many times."

"And her expertise on the accordion, let's not forget. Well, you'll not believe this but she has convinced me to help her with a situation in some English village. I leave this Monday morning."

"Great heavens, Rose. Have you lost your mind? No telling what that woman will have you doing. You are many things, Rose, but you are no scientist."

"I'm no scientist but I do know people. You're forgetting that Amaryllis was a genius in some areas but practically hopeless with one-on-one relationships with people."

"You are right there, Rose. That is exactly why she has asked you to join her. You are the kindest and most sympathetic person I've ever encountered."

"Now, Charlie—"

"Don't 'Now Charlie' me, Rose. I mean that."

"And another thing: Amaryllis has left Dr. Winslow Knebaard. She's probably lonely."

"Right again, Rose. Just don't let her walk over you. She can be very imperious as I recall. Now, is there anything at all I can do for you while you're gone? Or before you leave?"

Rose chuckled. Curious that Annie and Father Charlie used the same description when remembering Amaryllis: imperious.

෬෧෧ඏ

News of Rose's adventure spread lightning fast throughout Wynfield Farms. Those long-charmed by everything English were envious and eager to hear more details. Those few who did not share an affinity for "Anglophilia" or had never had a zest for travel were, frankly, bored. But everyone remembered Dr. Frances Keynes-Livingston: some with humor, some with awe, but all with great respect for the woman's education and versatile accomplishments. Her pearls were *always* a big point of discussion.

The Puffenbarger twins insisted on bringing a small, plain box to Rose's door, "to slip into your carry-on, for Dr. Frances. It's a new battery-operated magnifying glass that she can carry while in the field."

Father Charlie stopped by with a worn and well-loved P.D. James mystery. "You'll want to read this first, Rose," he said with humor. "It's your kind of story."

Large and small kindnesses bestowed on Rose convinced her once again that Wynfield Farms was "home with a heart". *Heaven help us if they start using that as an advertisement!*

One of Rose's first calls after her tickets arrived on Saturday morning was to Jocey Ribble, the "go-to woman of all works" at Wynfield. Jocey had ferried countless residents to operas, parties and medical appointments, as well as train stations and airports.

Rose hesitated before asking, "Jocey, do you still have relatives near Charlotte? Yes? Would you like to pay them a visit this Monday morning? After dropping me at the Charlotte airport? Wonderful! I'll see you at 6:00 A.M. in the lobby."

Rose McNess was about to begin her adventure.

ဆၜၖ

"Welcome aboard, Madam! Let me show you to your seat."

Rose McNess smiled at the friendly flight attendant greeting her as she stepped aboard Flight 3025 at Charlotte-Douglas International Airport.

"My dear, you certainly don't have to look for your seat: you are in our First Class section. Here we are, '3A', by the window. May I put your bag overhead? And your raincoat? I assure you, Ms. McNess, you will be most comfortable. You'll have a delightful seatmate soon. He's a frequent flyer with us and always requests this seat. And he *always* boards at the last minute. One of the busy executives, I suppose…"

"Thank you, Miss. You've been very helpful."

As the attendant left to shepherd more incoming passengers, Rose McNess sank back into her seat and closed her eyes.

Why did I let Amaryllis talk me into this? She's the expert on moss or whatever. Lichen: I must learn to respect her field of expertise. I don't think I have thought about lichen since she left Wynfield Farms. She really is a bona fide lichenologist. Not many of those around. What a puzzle that woman is. Wonder when she left Australia? And what happened to that new husband? Oh, I have so many questions. She has a lot of explaining to do. And especially about the situation she has gotten us into. Rather bizarre, come to think of it. And even more bizarre that she has gotten me to be her sidekick.

Rose sat quietly in her seat, feet resting squarely on the floor of the plane. Her hands, still sensibly swathed in black gloves, clasped a battered black purse. She glanced at her watch.

Is it just 5:40? Oh Golly! Well, another half-hour before we fly. The children think me foolish, but I am glad I got to the airport three hours before departure. I've had too many near-misses between Roanoke and Charlotte. Surely international flights try to leave on time.

Glancing around, Rose saw several families boarding, a few singles, and the usual clutch of college students. She wondered, was I ever that young? Backpack on my shoulders, no worries, no money, no cell phone! How did I even keep in touch with my parents? Old fashioned letters. We wrote in those days, on thin blue airmail paper that we bought in a real post office and stamped with real stamps if we could figure out the correct postage. What a trial. I hope these young people realize how lucky they are! And realize what incredible adventures await them at every corner. If they'll only take their eyes off their phones long enough to look!

Raucous laughter exploded through the plane. Another student, purple hair caught in two flopping ponytails, nose ring in place, hurriedly dodged past standing passengers to embrace her waiting friends.

Exchange students, Rose guessed, if I'm not mistaken. Off to indulge in the many pleasures of London or the continent. So pretty and fresh they are! But why do the young insist on piercings? Makes one feel quite old just looking at them. Here sits Rose the relic, an advertisement for every Senior Citizen League. Hair thin, short and gray, face round and wrinkled. But by golly, my eyes don't miss much! And I am a sturdy walker even if I must hustle to keep up with Amaryllis and her long legs.

Rose's thoughts returned again to Amaryllis.

How did she put it? A call at five in the morning, begging me to join her in London. Not asking, *begging, pleading,* for me to help solve a mystery in some English hamlet. Oh, she played on my love of everything English. Didn't let up. We'd travel by car to wherever, stay in charming inns, and I would assist her when it came to the investigation. What *sort* of investigation? Why did I agree to this? At my age.

Rose hugged her purse and closed her eyes. She pictured Frances Keynes-Livingston, the tall, patrician matron she had promptly dubbed 'Amaryllis' at their first encounter at Wynfield Farms. Indeed, with her swan-like neck (always caressed with a single strand of large and luminous pearls, pearls so large one knew they had to be the real thing) and statuesque bearing, she owned the nickname. But only when addressed thus by Rose. My closest confidante. Funny, quick, always willing to pull out her old accordion to play for folks. That was a real surprise: a *grande dame* toting a large instrument around her neck! What fun we had. Wonder what happened to the fellow from Australia . . . a doctor: yes, a doctor.

"Flight 3025, London, Heathrow, all passengers take seats. Door closing in five minutes."

Rose looked up quickly; her seatmate had still not arrived.

Oh, my goodness, here we go. First class! And roundtrip! How many times have I crossed the Atlantic . . . but never first class! Frances does things in style, including sending me these tickets. Spending her money on me . . . how could I turn her down? What do the Brits say: 'in for a penny, in for a pound'? Well, I'm the penny and Frances is the pound. This is so darned mysterious . . . and I'm going to enjoy it!

"May I take your order for something to drink? Champagne? Orange juice? Water? Beverage service begins as soon as we take off. Anything to make your travel more comfortable?"

"Thank you, Miss. I am just fine. Enjoying the perks of first class."

"Well done! You'll have company soon, Ms. McNess."

Amaryllis certainly knows how to spoil one. Every woman on this plane is a 'Ms.' to the attendants. They are here to shepherd us across the ocean. I can't make a fuss but I do prefer Mrs. McNess: My married title is important to me.

A loud guffaw and Rose looked up to see her seatmate arriving, jovially conversing with the attendant as if he had all the time in the world. He was a gentleman of indeterminate age, neither young nor old, neither fat or slim, and owning an expression of polite bemusement. He bowed slightly and offered Rose his hand before sliding into his seat.

"Thomas Ethridge. How do you do?"

"Mrs. Rose McNess. Very well, thank you, and looking forward to our flight."

"It will be swift and smooth, I assure you. Always pleasant."

"You sound as if you've made this trip many times," said Rose, smiling. She scrutinized him carefully. Very well turned out. Wonderful tweed jacket, leather-lined lapels, too! Liberty of London tie: that's appropriate. Why must I always suspect there is more to a person than what we see? Nice face, square chin. Thin lips: I never liked thin lips. Good eyes, more greenish than brown. Didn't look at me while we talked, not directly anyway. But very proper; can't fault him in that regard. Silly of me to waste time thinking so much about him. We are simply strangers on a plane. Strangers in the night.

"Oh, I've taken this same flight many times. I do a bit of import-export business in the British Isles, so this is just as familiar to me as driving from New York to Connecticut."

Probably Greenwich. Mr. Ethridge from Greenwich, Rose imagined.

"Well, as you may have guessed, First Class is a first for me. And I'm already enjoying it tremendously."

"*Au contraire.* You look every bit the seasoned traveler. Very comfortable up here where you belong. I'm sorry, I didn't get your name … Ms.?"

"*McNess.* Mrs. Rose McNess. I do prefer Mrs. I am too old to be a Ms.. From Virginia. And I promise I will not talk your ear off all the way over the Atlantic. I have much to think about as we cross the pond."

"As do I. This will be a longer flight for me. I had business in Charlotte today so I flew in from New York first thing. Usually leave from JFK. I'll sleep well. May I suggest a martini when our 'Girl Friday' returns? From past experience, I can tell you that a martini will do amazing things to ease your travel time! And your thoughts!"

With a final swoop, British Airways 3025 gently glided onto the runway at Heathrow. Rose, awakened by the flight attendant a half-hour before landing, freshened her hair, sighed at her wrinkles and devoured the juice and croissant waiting at her elbow.

"Sleep well, Mrs. McNess? You see, I did remember."

Rose smiled. "Like a rock, Mr. Ethridge. But then I always do. Sleep is a commodity that does not often elude me."

"Same here. A very comfortable night. Do you have someone meeting you at Heathrow or may I summon a cab for your convenience?"

"You are kind, but my friend is meeting me."

"Well done. If that's the case, I'm sure you will be well taken care of during your stay in London."

"I hope so. I'm here on a job. Not a *real* job, but I'm going to help my friend with her . . . plans. To be honest, I'm not sure what I am getting into. It will be an adventure; of that I *am* certain!"

Rose saw Mr. Ethridge taking her measure and was wondering just what sort of a job a woman her age would be undertaking. *If he only knew!* "I admire your spirit, Mrs. McNess. I wish you great success in your forthcoming challenge."

Mr. Ethridge smiled and retrieved a pen and small black notebook from his jacket. He frowned, bent close to the seat tray and began writing hurriedly, glancing from one page to another.

Rose, amused at her seatmate's sudden intensity, watched silently, then ventured, "Many appointments in London, Mr. Ethridge?"

"Not as many as usual. But the ones I must attend are important. Don't want to seem rude but I have names that are imperative for me to remember. If I don't jot them down beforehand, I'm hopeless. My business, you could say, is intensely international. And to be honest, Mrs. McNess, my memory is not always intensely accurate."

"I'm impressed, Mr. Ethridge. Of course, I admit to being somewhat older than you, but *my* memory is like a sieve—"

Thomas Ethridge laughed. "Don't sell yourself short, Mrs. McNess. Our problems seem to be similar. You need one of these pens. I'd be lost without the damn thing."

He showed her the notes he had written. Rose looked at a blank page.

"But there is nothing—"

"That's the beauty of it. It looks blank to you, but when I hold it in a certain light, all the writing reappears. Faint, but it appears."

Thomas Ethridge slanted the paper slightly and showed it to Rose. Names became legible.

"Amazing!"

"I picked this pen up in Munich. Frankly, I'd be lost without it. Must be some chemical in the ink. I'm able to scribble ten names on my nametag, give it a glance and *seem* to know each person's name at my meetings. When basically, I'm a bumbling idiot. Please don't give me away, Mrs. McNess."

"Your secret is safe with me."

And with that, both parties awaited the plane's final taxi to the gate. Flight attendants ushered first class passengers toward the exit. Amid spirited calls of "Goodbye, thank you for flying with British Airways," Rose McNess and Thomas Ethridge waved, smiled and headed into the terminal.

Chapter Two

"Rose! Rose! Over here!"

Frances Keynes-Livingston, taller by a head than most waiting for the disembarking hordes, waved her arms as Rose emerged from Customs Control. Rose, grinning broadly waved back, and hurried to embrace her friend. Dumping her bag, Rose reached up and hugged Frances enthusiastically, all the while exclaiming, "I can't believe I'm here! I can't believe *we're* here . . . together, in London! Look at you, pearls and all! You look marvelous, simply marvelous Amaryllis!"

"As do you, my love. Gracious, Rose, how long has it been? Three years? My brain cannot keep track of time. What matters is that we *are* together!"

"Oh, Amaryllis, it is wonderful to see you again. I worried all the way over the Atlantic about *what I* would call you . . . your very formal 'Frances' or the one I remember with such fondness from Wynfield Farms. You have not changed one bit. And your pearls—as beautiful as ever. You *are* my dear Amaryllis!"

The two friends hugged, oblivious to the commotion swirling around them. They were secure in the knowledge that having found each other once more, it would take more than a continent to separate their friendship, much less other travelers running for taxies.

"Come on, Rose. Is *that* all your luggage? One carry-on? Well done, love! Let's exit this way; I have a car waiting, we'll chatter all the way into London. I've booked us a room at the Currie Street and you may sleep the day away if you desire."

"Ah, the Currie Street! You would! You *know* it's my favorite. I thought perhaps it had gone the way of so many other small hotels."

"Not the Currie. Same staff, same glorious teas, same elegant beds."

"I slept all the way over, Amaryllis. Well, most of the way. And I don't plan to waste the day sleeping. I am simply dying to learn why my presence is required on this case of yours. *I confess I did tell Annie, and hinted to a few of our fellow confederates.* The boys think I have taken myself over to Britain to see spring arrive! They know how dreary March can be at home. But I am just about to pop with curiosity!"

"All shall be revealed, Rose. By the time we fight our way into the city, you'll be ready for a nap. Even if it's brief. And then I shall spill all my secrets. Oh, take a look at this while I get us out of Heathrow." She handed Rose a neatly clipped notice detailing her recent lecture at London University.

"Whew, I am impressed! Good crowd?"

"Packed!"

❦

Manager and staff alike at The Currie Street Hotel hurried to the small lobby to personally welcome Rose and Amaryllis.

"Gracious! I didn't expect such a welcoming committee," exclaimed Rose, smiling at the beaming staff eager to take her coat, carry her bag and generally make her feel at home once more in London.

"It has been too long, Mrs. McNess," intoned Cyril. "As I recall it has been over three years since we last saw you. And that was when half your fellow residents came along, also."

"It must have *seemed* half of Wynfield Farms, Cyril. There were just ten, or eleven, as I recall. Were we so rowdy that you remember us that well?"

"Not rowdy, Mrs. McNess. Let us just say you were a spirited group of—"

"Go ahead, say it: Old Age Pensioners. OAPs! In the States we're called 'Senior Citizens'!"

"So be it. Your group was most welcome. And high-spirited. Ian will show you to your room. Your friend has reserved the suite on three for your comfort. I am certain you will be pleasantly situated. A light tea is on its way to welcome you. If there is anything else, please let us know."

"Tea sounds perfect . . . if the bed doesn't claim me first! Thank you so much, Cyril. I feel as if I am home already!" Rose and Amaryllis followed Ian to the lift and to their suite.

Ian settled Rose's luggage on the large rack and at Amaryllis's request closed the mauve shades to bar the daylight from the traveler's eyes. After ensuring the tea table was adequately positioned, Ian departed with silence and a smile.

"Oh, Amaryllis, let me undo my shoes and join you for a cuppa. And one of the Currie's divine pastries. This suite is lovely! Why, we could even entertain a—"

"Rose! No entertaining on this trip! At least not yet. WE are our own party. I do love plenty of room for stretching out, however. I believe they call this suite the 'Lounge'. Whatever, it's lovely. Here's your tea. Sugar?"

"Not this morning, dear. Hot and steaming, period. Now before we get into the mystery at hand, catch me up on your glamorous life in Melbourne. And if I fall asleep, pinch me."

Frances Keynes-Livingston, *aka* Amaryllis, never known to act in haste, slowly and deliberately told Rose of her life with, and without, Dr. Winslow Knebaard in Melbourne, Australia.

"Our careers just got in the way of love, Rose," admitted Amaryllis.

Wistfully thought Rose, as she watched her friend's face.

"We had many tender moments, but they were followed by catch-ups, frantic hours at the labs, and then trying to come together again. After two years, we came to a simultaneous conclusion that we were better partners in academia than partners in bed. Or marriage. A very amicable divorce followed and, well, here I am."

Rose remained silent, shook her head thoughtfully, then asked quickly, "And who proposed this terrific proposition that has brought me halfway round the world to assist you? And where are we *going? I* will not leave my chair until you spill the beans."

Amaryllis smiled her Cheshire cat smile and reached over to take Rose's cup before it slipped from her friend's hand. Rose's eyes closed as she drifted into slumber.

"East Plumley, Rose. We are going to East Plumley."

Chapter Three

Rose opened her eyes in the early afternoon to find her head nestled on a down pillow and herself propped in a chair, still in traveling clothes, under a duvet that more resembled cloud than comforter. The tea tray had vanished. Amaryllis sat at the writing desk by the window, hands flying over the keys of her laptop.

"All right, old friend. You've had your way. And of course, I feel better after that snooze. Did I dream it, or were the last words I heard before drifting off 'East Plumley'?"

"You heard correctly. East Plumley is our destination, and don't ask me where it is! I'm surprised you remembered: you've been out for about four hours. It's nearly time for tea again."

"Please, dear heart, no more tea. Would it suit you just as well to wait until dinner? Then we could have our drinks and really relax. I think they begin serving at seven o'clock and by then I could manage a real Currie meal. How about it, Amaryllis?"

"Perfect! That's why we get on so well, Rose. We are of the same mind on so many things. Big *and* small, not only the hour to dine."

"Agreed. Let me freshen up a bit; it's time to talk."

Amaryllis turned off her laptop and slid the heavy draperies to one side. Daylight was rapidly fading and soon London's city lights would be winking through the veil of branches fronting Currie Street.

"All right," declared Rose, returning to her chair. "Amaryllis, I am still waiting."

They laughed and then Amaryllis started, "Before I begin telling you of the epic journey upon which we are about to embark, I simply must ask you, Rose, about your lovely friend, David. I did share a barebones account of *my* marital chapter. What about your long-running romance with the most gorgeous guide in the United Kingdom?"

Rose blushed. "Not much to tell, really. David did visit Wynfield several times, or did I write you about that? I keep forgetting you were in Australia for two years."

"Three. Continue, Rose. Did you rekindle your friendship when he visited?"

"We had a lovely time. He thoroughly enjoyed his visits to Virginia and I enjoyed the tours we did in Europe."

"Persiflage! You are not telling me the whole story! Will you see him while you're over here?"

Rose giggled, a decidedly un-lady-like giggle, half-muffled by the small pillow she clasped in front of her face.

"You're blushing, Rose! You can't hide it from Amaryllis!"

"You're right: I'm guilty. But isn't blushing good for the complexion? And to answer your question, yes, we have arranged to meet after this little foray. Date to be decided, depending on completion of our mission. Which leads me to ask, just what *is* our mission?"

"In good time. But one more question. You have never looked better: are you feeling quite sexy at the moment? Anticipating David?"

"Amaryllis!"

"I mean that as a compliment, Rose. You look incredibly sexy for a—"

"For a woman of indeterminate age? Well, I *do* thank you, Amaryllis."

"Then all I have to say is, go for it, Rose! My late-blooming romance with Winslow was terrific. Until work managed to get in the way. But I told you all that. And we're still mad about each other. If we are in the same room, it's as if we are two magnets. We are unavoidably, inescapably *drawn* to one another, even though we can't seem to live in the same flat."

"They do say that attention from the opposite sex helps one live longer."

"And healthier."

"Even puts roses, *not* wrinkles, on one's cheeks."

"And stars in the eyes."

The pair laughed until they cried, then, wiping tears away, Rose persisted.

"Enough, Amaryllis. Two questions for you."

"Fair enough. I'll allow you two."

"Amaryllis, those gorgeous pearls of yours, are they the real thing?"

"My lips are sealed."

"All right. Tell me what is taking us to East Plumley, wherever that is."

"Ready, dear? I may get long-winded and a bit technical. If so, just stop me. I was in the Melbourne apartment packing the last case when the phone rang. Who should be on the line but Dr. Thailman, one of my Cambridge professors. You remember I did some post-doc work there—"

"Of course." Amaryllis' academic credentials were, to Rose's mind, almost legendary. "Continue."

"Seems the professor is on a committee to preserve churchyards in England. It's a sub-committee of the British Lichen Society based in Cambridge."

Rose interrupted: "Preserve churchyards? As in gardening?"

"Patience! Dr. Thailman had just received a troubling phone call from one of his old classmates at Cambridge who is presently a vicar in East Plumley. Seems someone has been stealing the gravestones from his churchyard. Can you believe the audacity of such an act?"

"Neither the audacity nor the time and labor involved. But why, and how does this concern the preservation committee?"

"Hear me out, Rose. Lichenologists know that many of the gravestones in the English churchyards are ancient. And I mean really ancient. In some places, centuries."

"And still standing out in the elements?"

"Absolutely. And covered with lichen. Tons of fascinating, beautiful lichen. Did you know there are over 1,800 known species of lichen within Britain? Incredible, but true. Churchyards all over the British Isles are being suffocated by poor air quality, shade from overgrown trees, and pollutants. Ecclesiastical property committee members go around the countryside examining the lichen in churchyards in order to study environmental effects. Then they suggest steps churches may take to correct the situation."

"Study the lichen? Is this church committee a censoring group? I envision tall professors in black coats and homburgs stomping around a churchyard and saying, 'This must go, that must go.'"

"Oh, no, no, no! Quite the contrary! Churches actually invite the committee to come and make suggestions. Churchyards are history; headstones are history. Lichen must thrive to continue the history. The committee's intent is to improve the environment for the artifacts and therefore preserve the lichen. Some can only thrive exactly where they are. In many instances, lichen are as individual to the site as a fingerprint is to a hand. Lichen can be used to identify a specific site."

"The vicar in East Plumley: do you think he has any idea of the importance of lichen in his churchyard, or is it just the fact that the headstones have been stolen?"

"I seriously doubt if the vicar is a trained scientist, but he obviously understands how the removal of three lichen laden gravestones would affect the ecological balance in the churchyard. And yes, I think he is greatly concerned, and rightly so, with these thefts."

"And your role as a lichenologist is?"

"To assess the lichen found in the churchyard of St. Michael's in the Cedars. Lichen is a complicated organism, composed of algae and fungus. The two parts are co-dependent: a symbiotic relationship. Lichen have been used for centuries in a variety of things, including traditional medicines, pigments and inks. Call it a sixth sense, call it what you will, but I think, and I think the vicar thinks, the thieves are after more than old headstones."

"I am amazed, Amaryllis. But why in the world do you need me? I know nothing about lichen. That's your department!"

"Rose, the two of us are *lichen*. *I* told you that lichens are composed of two parts: fungal elements and algae. Each depends upon its partner for survival. That is exactly the way we operate. We are co-dependent. And that's *why I* need you!"

"Oh, Amaryllis, I'm touched." Rose reached over and hugged her old friend.

"I need you, Rose, because you are everything I am not: practical, gracious with people, superbly organized. I look for facts. I can spot the lichen, identify it, slice it, distill it and be blind to the thief. Or thieves. You, Rose, are in charge of solving this mystery."

"'Rose, in charge'. I rather like the sound of that, Amaryllis."

Chapter Four

The next morning Rose and Amaryllis managed to depart the Currie Street Hotel by ten o'clock. Both were eager to avoid London's famously hectic morning traffic and the crush of entering the main northbound arteries. The highways teemed with automobiles and lorries speeding toward distant destinations. Amaryllis, indomitable, was fearless and familiar with left-side-of-the-road driving. Although reassured by her friend's driving skills, Rose nevertheless felt obliged to keep keen eyes trained on the path ahead.

"You're doing a superb job of navigating, Amaryllis. Will my talking distract you? I don't want to be a bother."

"Bother? Never, Rose. Let me pass this van and then chat away. We have at least four or five hours of driving ahead of us. Some of these roads are less than super highways, but after York, we'll catch the M-l. That will speed us along. Plenty of time to catch up on everything."

Startled to realize she had been frozen to the edge of her seat since leaving their hotel, Rose felt her shoulders relax as she settled back in the seat and considered her position. Amaryllis is an excellent driver and not the least intimidated by the perils of English motorways. She really is quite a woman. Certainly she's my age or even a few years older… but what zest for life. She's jumped right into this mystery as chief investigator as if she has been just waiting for a challenge. She may have put me in charge, but she's still leading the hunt.

"Amaryllis, do you ever think of Wynfield Farms? And miss it just a little bit?"

"Oh, I certainly do think of it. Wynfield Farms was more than a 'retirement home.' Everyone there, well *almost* everyone, was so active and engaged. It was, for lack of a better description, a resort for independent seniors. It was akin to being on a cruise that never ended, nor did we want it to end. Those were my idyllic years. I vegetated. Happily, I might add. And to find you, dear friend, was well, serendipitous."

"Feeling's mutual, I assure you. And Australia? Any regrets there?"

"The country is amazing, Rose. I wish you had the time to fly out from here. You'd be overcome with the beauty of the landscape. And the people. They are so warm and welcoming."

"A little far-flung from home for this trip, dear. Now, for starters, what do you know about East Plumley? I've never heard of the town. And I don't see it on the ordnance map, either."

"Not surprised. The population is, according to the vicar, 'around six hundred, with increases on market days and high season'. It's in the northeast quadrant of Britain, not far from the coast, should one want to summer near the North Sea. We'll probably see gobs of rain while we're there."

"Six hundred. And there's this sinister business going on in the town. Sorry, go on dear."

"I should imagine East Plumley is fairly typical of small villages one sees all over Great Britain. Tidy, tightly contained, a major 'high street' with charming shops, one inn, one pub. Dormers, gables, stonework, that sort of thing."

"Did you say *one* inn? I guess they don't expect many tourists."

"Well, the towns of Ely and Swaffham are relatively close. Tourists would flock to the larger towns for their specific attractions and I am sure B&B's and hotels are plentiful in both towns. I would doubt if East Plumley has a police station either. The smaller towns in Great Britain usually don't. Maybe a local constable, but not a police force."

"And the one inn? Did you make reservations for the two of us?"

"Not to worry, Rose: the vicar has taken care of our accommodations. I think we shall be very comfortable."

"You've talked to him? How did he sound, ancient?"

"In a word, *worried*. And no, not ancient. In truth, a lovely distinctive voice. Quiet, well-modulated as only the Brits can be. His name is wonderful: Coulton S. Ellington. If I had to bet, the two of us are some years older than he. The curate is a Mr. Blakely; no first name given. Apparently, the curate is fairly new to the parish, but that may be relative: the vicar said he'd been there sixteen years."

"I'm taking notes. Vicar, Ellington. Curate, Blakely. And the name of the parish again?"

"St. Michael's in the Cedars. Established 1789. And that is where the vicar discovered our crimes."

"Please, Amaryllis! I don't want it to be 'our crimes', yet. Do you have any idea what size St. Michael's is? I ask because that might give us an idea of the size of the graveyard."

"None whatsoever. But it cannot be very grand because East Plumley is but a village. If it was built in the mid-18th Century, its architecture is bound to be Georgian with perhaps a smattering of Regency."

Rose was silent, trying to recall notes from her Wellesley History of Architecture classes sixty years ago. "You realize, Amaryllis, my memory is not what it used to be. Flighty as a thistle in the wind. But I'm visualizing a simple stone church with a classical portico and a steeple above. Probably rows of box pews in the nave on either side of a central aisle."

"I knew I needed an art historian with me. Tell me, by your calculations, will there be any stained-glass in St. Michael's?"

"Not sure about that. But probably so, as by the 12th century stained-glass was a sophisticated art form in England. There's even a stained-glass museum in Ely. Probably a simple interior, raised altar. And perhaps a 'bonnet' over the lectern."

"'Bonnet'?"

"In some English churches, they call them 'canopies' or 'sounding boards' or, sometimes, 'testers'. I've read about a fabulous stained glass bonnet in an old church in York. If St. Michael's has one, it is certainly not famous."

"Personally, I prefer 'bonnet' to 'canopy'. Bonnet lifts my spirits; canopy sounds funereal, and tester is even worse."

"I am looking forward to our adventure, Amaryllis. Wonder if East Plumley is ready for the two of us! Now about those thefts…"

"To continue, the vicar was walking in his churchyard a couple of weeks ago and stumbled over two large depressions. Literally *stumbled*. He realized at once that headstones had been removed. And then a few days later one more hollow was discovered in a far corner. The holes had been filled and covered with leaves and other debris but the depressions were deep enough to cause him to stumble. That same week one of his parishioners called to tell him that her gate stop had gone missing."

"A gate stop?"

"One of those balls attached to a chain on the back of a gate to insure a proper closing. Ridiculous? Why or how would a person go to the trouble to steal that?"

"Lichen?" ventured Rose.

Amaryllis continued, undeterred by the large bus she was passing.

"Both instances nagged at the good vicar, so much so that he called the Church of England offices in Cambridge. He described the objects as headstones covered in lichen. That triggered the churchyard group that works with lichens and stones and Thailman's call to yours truly."

"This is becoming more and more intriguing. You will be doing scientific study at St. Michael's and I shall be doing the same at the pub. I can't think about pubs without remembering our experience in London years ago when one of the Puffenbarger twins disappeared!"

"And was found napping at the V & A! My glory, Rose, that nearly ended your career as guide for the Wynfield crowd."

"And now I reinvent myself as a sleuth, huh?"

"You'll be perfect, Rose. The pub is where you'll meet all the town's characters, good, bad and indifferent. Plus, pick up all the latest gossip."

"We'll have to think up a cover story, Amaryllis. Maybe we are part of a world-wide church survey team, traveling the world to see how religious establishments with a high percentage of seniors thrive in an endangered world. Does that sound too flimsy?"

"Marvelous, Rose. I bet that folks in East Plumley would leap at a chance to tell you everything you needed to know about their little village. But all this talk about pubs has made me long for a tall lemonade and a small sandwich. What do you say we turn off at the first promising roundabout and satisfy our hunger?"

Chapter Five

Amaryllis and Rose turned off the M-l, followed the roundabout to the final exit and drove slowly into East Plumley.
The village clock straight ahead read exactly two minutes before three o'clock in the afternoon. The signal light at the
town's main entrance was red. Amaryllis stopped, affording
both driver and passenger a good look at their destination.
With a sky as blue as a Dutchman's breeches and a lemony
sun that bathed everything below in a golden and glorious
light, East Plumley looked the storybook English village. The
Union Jacks along High Street fluttered in a gentle breeze,
their brilliant reds and blues competing with the sharp green
of merchants' awnings and Gulliver-size pots of red gerani-
ums surely not out a week. East Plumley seemed to have di-
versified, even expanded, while maintaining its quota of tried
and true staples. Names ranged from the poetic to the practical: Mary's Own (tea shop), One or More (bakery), AGE-
LESS ANTIQUES, and Bibbs' (green grocer). Set among the

shops was one Indian establishment, for who among the British does not enjoy a pungent curry? Shop windows sparkled and it appeared that the grass-green awnings were sturdy and new. Sidewalks held a scattering of pedestrians at this hour; those present were busy gossiping with one another or making their way to specific destinations. Tea time was approaching and folks kept priorities in mind.

Midway along the eastern side of the High, The Plumley Arms, stalwart and venerable, reigned supreme in its position as the town's one hostelry. A branch of NationWide Building Society (successor to the long-departed Barclay's) stood opposite the Arms. Townspeople and visitors alike viewed the NationWide and the Arms buildings good naturedly, with a nod to their grandiose appearance. With grave and gray weathered stone facades faithful to Georgian architectural style, they quietly dominated their lesser neighbors along the street.

The Rose and Thistle, situated a mere thirty yards along the High from the Arms, distinguished itself by being East Plumley's one public house. Its claim held that the first proprietors of the Arms had insisted that this 'goodly distance be established' between their establishment and the public house, less any 'rancorous merriment disturb the sanctity and sleep of guests'. Weather had faded the colors of 'The Rose' sign, yet it swayed jauntily, even defiantly, above the narrow blue door that was, at this time of the day, firmly closed.

Rose looked toward the village green. At the far end of High Street, St. Michael's in the Cedars appeared to be slumbering, encircled by a sensuous cluster of majestic cedars. Its simple spire, bronze cross atop, punctuated the afternoon sky with authority as it gleamed in the sunshine. The location of the compact church looked convenient to shoppers seeking shady rest in warm weather or refuge from rain and winter cold. Thanks to a succession of dedicated caregivers during the church's long history, St. Michael's wrought iron fence and lyche gate hinges glistened with a new coat of black paint. There was no doubt that the hinges were well-oiled and that bulletins were promptly posted and/or removed from the standing board opposite. The fact that St. Michael's churchyard was under suspicion and study was due not to neglect by the present caretaker, but by the perpetrators of a fiendish crime.

❧

"No wonder the fellow behind me is annoyed: I keep forgetting the damn signals on these British autos. Not to worry, we're here at last." Amaryllis manuvered the car into the gravel area marked 'car park'.

"I like the looks of this already. Here, let me take that extra bag." Rose grabbed the blue duffel.

"You mean my *forensic* bag: tools of the trade."

"I'll be doubly careful, *Sherlock*. Thank goodness we both know how to travel: not an extra ounce between us."

"Another one of your many virtues, Rose. Isn't this a lovely entrance? I like the way they direct one through this mundane vehicular stable and around to the front entrance. Would you call this pseudo-Georgian architecture, dear?"

Rose and Amaryllis paused to glance admiringly at the warm gray stones of the Arms as they walked the short distance to the front. The broad oak door swung open at their approach, with no evidence of effort save the tips of white gloves sighted at the edge of the massive portal. This mystery was quickly solved by a voice from within.

"Greetings, Mesdames! Welcome to The Plumley Arms. Dr. Keynes-Livingston and Mrs. Rose McNess. Am I correct?"

The welcome came booming into the foyer with the force of a rocket. Both women smiled spontaneously as they searched for the source of the voice. "Oh, my," whispered Rose, "Are you sure we're not in a National Trust house?"

At a glance the Plumley Arms lobby was indeed impressive. High ceilings and tall windows assured full light. Burnished pine mantle and moldings enhanced the spacious room while a vibrant cobalt blue provided accents of color on a scattering of settees and chairs. These rested on a worn Shiraz covering a generous portion of the floor.

"I am Giles, concierge of The Plumley Arms. At your

service, Mesdames." Giles slid from behind the dimly lit door and extended a gloved hand to each.

Rose and Amaryllis deposited their meager luggage and shook the proffered hand.

"Pleasant drive from London, I presume?"

"Absolutely. We drifted off course a bit near Ely. Spot of sightseeing and a good lunch. Can't resist a tasty ploughman! We're happy to be here in East Plumley, and at the Arms, which certainly exceeds the description I was given." This from Amaryllis in her prime first business-then-pleasure voice.

"Thank you, Madam. If you will do us the courtesy of signing the register, Kevin will escort you to your suite. I've given you one at the front. I think you will be extremely comfortable. If there is any concern, I shall be happy to assist you."

"A suite at the front sounds fine. Thank you so much."

Rose, Amaryllis and Kevin filled the small but efficient lift and were on the next level before Rose had a chance to speak to the timid porter. Kevin appeared to be in his late teens, highly nervous, and poured into a uniform obviously designed for a person of a slighter build than he.

Rose began planning her investigations. She'd make a point of forgetting something in the morning and hope for a chance to speak to Kevin. It looked as if he could be a talker. She might as well start her snooping here at the Arms.

Rose and Amaryllis stood silently behind the young man as he unlocked the door to their suite. Amaryllis thanked him graciously as he deposited their bags, smiled, and backed swiftly through the door.

"Would you look at our suite, Amaryllis? Each of us with a room of our own plus this—a party room! I'm smitten with The Arms' blue and beige color scheme. It has a very, well, calming effect, don't you agree?"

"Do you think we'll need calming, dear?"

"One never knows with this mystery of yours."

"OURS, Rose. OUR mystery, and I've put you in charge, in case you've forgotten in your swoon over the color scheme."

"Never fear, Amaryllis. That nice young man who brought our bags: do you recall his name? Wait, I've got it: Kevin. Yes, Kevin. Nice young man. I'll have a chat with him."

"You do that, Rose, but right now I'm going to change my shoes. Want to walk down to St. Michael's with me? Can't be far; nothing is too distant in East Plumley."

"Including devious criminals." murmured Rose. "Hmm… some interesting brochures here on the table. And the light is even bright enough to read them. Now that is a rarity in any hotel. Golly, here's one with rentals. Perhaps I'll rent a bicycle for my exploring."

"Rose, forget *that!* Shoes on please."

"Listen to this Amaryllis."

"I'm listening as I throw on another sweater. Go ahead."

"There's a well-illustrated pamphlet about the local pub. I'll just…"

"Not all, Rose. Your shoes please. We need to get to St. Michael's while the light is still good."

"Just this then: 'In 1785 a gentleman from Norfolk named Josiah Benham wandered into East Plumley, staked out a parcel of land on the High to' -I love this!- 'to establish and maintain the sole and proper place in East Plumley towne to serve plaine food and drink to gentlemen and ladies be they stopped or traveling.' There's more. 'Benham's words were included in the original charter of East Plumley when the town was incorporated in 1787. Thus the Rose and Thistle reigns supreme.' Wonderful."

"So it is. But get your shoes on, Rose, and let's hustle on down to the High."

Chapter Six

Rose and Amaryllis, wearing extra sweaters and comfortable shoes, walked down to reception and placed their key in Giles' waiting hand.

"Our suite is perfect, Giles. Thank you so very much."

"Had orders from the vicar: 'Very important guests arriving today and I want them situated in The Arms' finest'." Giles smiled benignly at his role in the Vicar's instructions.

"Well, best we get on to St. Michael's and assume our important role. Onward, Rose!"

"Ladies may I have a word before you depart?"

Both ladies snapped to attention at Giles' exhortation. His deep voice was as somber as his expression. Did he think Rose and Amaryllis were enemies breaching a moat?

He's an ancient Roman senator, thought Rose, quietly observing the lean, upright man behind the voice. Sparse gray hair slicked over a rounded skull; not a wisp escaped. Hooded lids shuttered faded clear blue eyes from which no detail was hidden. With his large Roman nose, Giles was the image of a classical statue. He's a warrior battling for his cause. Of course! The Plumley Arms is his cause and we must be his good soldiers. Or else…

Rose's observations were interrupted by the old warrior, who stopped shuffling a sheaf of papers he had been holding.

"Keys will be deposited with me upon leaving the Arms. They shall reside securely in this cubicle. Housekeeping details are enumerated in the packet in your suite and matron is available at all times if you should have need. Breakfast is in the salon, 0600 to 0900." Here Giles allowed himself a small chuckle as his lips creased slightly.

"Any other queries, I'll be more than happy to address. I am at your service to assure you a pleasant and memorable visit in East Plumley."

With that the two ladies breezed out the entrance and began their inspection of the village of East Plumley.

"Would you call Giles a bit officious, Amaryllis? I would love to sneak off and keep my key. Just to get his goat. What a character"

"I agree, Rose, but he may be a hidden asset in this investigation. We'll humor him and return his keys. For the time being, anyway. Certainly the vicar didn't tell him *why* we're here. Always best to operate clandestinely, wouldn't you agree?"

"Absolutely. Perhaps Giles suspects that we're 'church ladies'. You know, meeting with the vicar about world surveys and so forth. Oh, be still my heart! Would you look at that pub, Amaryllis. And so close to the Arms.*"

'The Rose and Thistle: that is made for you, my dear. Especially since you *are* a church lady. And look across the High. It's small but it is in fact a BOOTS the Chemist. How convenient. Right next to what looks to be a hardware store. Didn't know the small, independent ones even stayed in business anymore."

"I am trying to take in everything, Amaryllis. Seems to be more than a fair number of shops."

"And a fair number of cats! There goes a gray one. It's the third I've seen so far."

"You know; I've been thinking about adopting a cat. It has been so lonely since Max died. And though a cat is not a Scottie, well, I take the presence of cats as an omen of a peaceful village. People who are kind to animals cannot be all evil."

"Oh, Rose, I wish I had your belief in the innate goodness of mankind. Don't forget why we are here in East Plumley."

"Not for a minute, Amaryllis, not for a minute. Leave it to me: I plan to explore every corner of this charming village. And of course the High leads straight to the green and the green to the church. Mystery or not, we are going to love East Plumley. I already do."

"Come on, you hopeless romantic!" cried Amaryllis. Laughing the pair linked arms and continued walking along High Street toward St. Michael's in the Cedars. As the two visitors strolled onto the Village Green, they caught their first full view of the church.

"Oh, Amaryllis, look! It's almost as I had visualized it: lovely mellow gray stone, tall steeple and a clerestory. Larger than I would have thought. But that porch!"

"I agree, Rose. It doesn't fit. Do you think it was an afterthought?"

"Probably a late addition to keep the congregation dry."

"The C of E doesn't want rain to discourage its worshippers. Rose—look, I believe the vicar is waiting for us."

"Oh, Golly," Rose whispered, "so he is."

Reverend Ellington could have stepped from central casting into the role of village priest. Tall, lean and ram-rod straight, Rose immediately told herself that he must have been a fine athlete at university. Closely cropped gray hair covering the beginning-to-bald pate added to the impression of athleticism. Decidedly dark blue eyes sparkled with intelligence even in the fading light and his broad smile belied any problems that had necessitated his call for assistance. He stooped slightly under the low cedar beams of St. Michael's *porte cochere* as he extended both hands in greeting.

"Ladies! Welcome! I've been expecting you, Dr. Keynes-Livingston, since talking to our colleague in Cambridge. So pleased that you've made time for us. And—"

"May I introduce my assistant, Vicar: Mrs. Rose McNess. Not only my assistant but a friend of long standing."

Reverend Ellington bowed slightly and offered his hand to both ladies.

"Welcome to East Plumley. I trust your drive from London was without incident? A bit hectic with all the lorries, I'm sure."

"Driving is not a problem for me, Vicar. And neither is the left."

"That's quite an art for some. Now, if you ladies are not too fatigued, I suggest we visit our churchyard while the afternoon light is clear. Rain is forecast for early evening so clouds will be moving in shortly. We'll have refreshments in my office a bit later, if that suits—"

"By all means. I am here to investigate. I want to look at the grounds *and* the remaining gravestones. I'll return in the morning to poke around more thoroughly, but I am eager to see where all this began."

'Poke around'! Little does the good vicar know what Amaryllis has in her investigation bag! She'll turn the churchyard into an 'Enter by Clerical Authority Only' zone. I know how she works!

The three turned right from the entrance of St. Michael's and entered the churchyard. A canopy of tall cedars waved in the slight breeze and shadows danced among rows of headstones. The spongy ground was thick with needles.

Amaryllis noted the green and yellow lichen edging the engravings of many stones. Rose, face turned to the sky, was fascinated by the height and density of the cedars.

"So peaceful here, Vicar," observed Rose. "And the aroma *is* positively intoxicating. Must seem like Yuletide every day."

The vicar smiled. "It *is* peaceful, isn't it? I come here daily in good weather. Just to meditate and appreciate the simple goodness of this place. Even after nearly three centuries the churchyard is still quite special despite the desecration." The vicar stopped suddenly and pointed to the two deep depressions at his feet.

"Dr. Keynes-Livingston, here is where the first missing headstones stood for more than two hundred years. This very spot until three weeks ago. Because it is rather a secluded corner, Botts didn't notice in his everyday maintenance. But on his weekly census it was immediately apparent. And then, of course, he reported it to me."

Both ladies raised inquisitive eyebrows.

"Sorry! That's Willem Botts, sexton, caretaker, man of all works. Let me have a look beyond this hedge. Yes, there's old Botts now. One can always spot him by that blue blazer; his daily uniform. Botts! I say, Botts! Could you spare us a moment please?"

The vicar turned to Rose and Amaryllis and whispered, "Man has to be over seventy but still strong as a workhorse. He's as distraught over this mischief as I."

Willem Botts, rake in hand, shambled through the hedge and joined the waiting trio. His cobalt-blue blazer glowed in the half-light of the cedars.

"Botts, may I present Dr. Livingston and Mrs. McNess. They are part of a church group that will be with us for several days. I've told them about your superb work and discovery of the first of the missing headstones."

A blush of scarlet spread across Botts' worn face as he removed his hat and nodded appreciatively at the vicar's recognition. He was undeniably proud of his position at the church.

"And the other stone was where? Could you point that out for us, please?"

Botts pointed to the far edge of the churchyard and said, "Right thar, next to the corner post. Careful the mounds and depressions 'long the way." He nodded his head slightly, turned, and retraced his steps to the hedgerow he had been cleaning.

Rose watched Botts retrace his steps and wondered if she'd be able to get the man to chat with her. *A character that one.*

The vicar continued the search. "Here, Doctor, next to the post. That stone dated from the 1780s. Stapleton family, if I recall. Old bachelor. This thievery saddens me."

Reverend Ellington detailed what Amaryllis had heard from her Cambridge colleague. Three stones in the churchyard removed, and two parishioners reported thefts of odd pieces of masonry 'lifted' from their yards in East Plumley and, finally, a heavy millstone out of the park by the river.

"Why would anyone take a gate stop? And who would lift a small grave marker from an obscure back garden? Indeed, it had marked an old spaniel's resting place. And the idea of a thief taking a small millstone by the town's stream was ludicrous. Cheap molded concrete, all three articles. Why, indeed?"

"I certainly share your feelings, Vicar. I've never been involved in a case this heinous. Those who disturb cemeteries show no regard for sanctity of life or soul. But I have learned one important fact this afternoon."

"And what is that, Dr. Keynes-Livingston?"

"Most of the stones remaining are of similar content: a common mixture that, in time, tends to crumble and disintegrate unless properly cared for, which I gather Botts does on a daily basis. Only one marble monument on site: that monstrous angel. The stones that were removed, and I am putting it politely, undoubtedly cracked into pieces once lifted from the ground. I don't care how carefully they were removed, their age betrayed them. There would be no resale value as an artifact. Reverend Ellington, I am convinced that the thieves were after more than headstones. These criminals may not have university degrees in the sciences but they knew what they were stealing. And why!"

"I am astounded, Doctor. Professor Thailman did not exaggerate your credentials. You have lifted my spirits ten-fold, even if I am still very troubled. I say, let's go warm ourselves and our souls with a dram of sherry!"

Chapter Seven

The vicar's office was cheerful and filled with light.

Two ample square windows, shutters pushed wide, filtered the late afternoon sun. Below the windows crowded bookcases held volumes that looked both well-thumbed and well-loved.

Sensing that Amaryllis would have questions for the vicar, Rose took a chair to the left of his desk and immediately began looking over the surroundings.

A worn Hamadan carpet in shades of red and indigo contributed a comfortable touch, as did three blue leather chairs surrounding the vicar's desk. The desk faced a rough stone fireplace crowned with a magnificent mantle of two-inch thick walnut, a plank polished to a high sheen. A small wood fire crackled in the grate and lent intimacy to the simple room.

Other than two photographs in traditional silver frames, a large monthly calendar, telephone and a Bible, the vicar's desk was bare.

Rose noted the lack of clutter in the room. Seems a well-organized sort. I do like that in a man. He's organized or is he just plain neat? Obviously, Amaryllis and I will compare opinions later.

Rose watched the Vicar as he carefully helped Amaryllis take off her jacket, and just as carefully placed it on the simple clothes tree in the corner. Next he removed his jacket, patted both pockets and arranged it next to Amaryllis' garment.

Was he looking for his keys? Pipe? Cigarettes? Old Giles just put keys on my mind. Thank goodness, the vicar is not a smoker, Rose thought to herself.

The vicar's gaze was steady and his expression serene. Every move he made was unhurried yet purposeful. He stood in front of the small fire, clasped his hands together and said in a hearty voice, "Ladies, I've suggested sherry but if that is not agreeable I'll call—"

"Sherry will be perfect, vicar," responded a smiling Amaryllis.

"And as if by magic, we have sherry!" laughed the vicar as the door was opened by a petite gnome of a woman with eyes the color of English bluebells. She carried a tray bearing a full decanter of Harvey's Bristol Cream, three small glasses and a plate of shortbread.

"Dr. Keynes-Livingston, Mrs. McNess, may I introduce my right arm, our cook and a vital component of St. Michael's, Mrs. Phil Pickett."

The cherubic gnome smiled in embarrassment as she left the tray and bustled quickly from the room.

The vicar poured sherry for each and raised his glass in a toast: "To my new American friends!"

"And I would add, to the rapid solution of this crime!"

"So right, Doctor…we shall drink to that."

"Rose and I will not disappoint, Reverend Ellington." The trio sipped quietly for a few moments, each deep in thought as they watched flames play on the small hearth.

Rose was the first to break the silence.

"St. Michael's is just what I had envisioned: small, sturdy, compact. And your office is lovely. It suits you. How long have you been here at St. Michael's, vicar?"

"Sixteen years, Mrs. McNess, seventeen in September. As you might guess, I spend more time here than at the vicarage. It's the quiet I enjoy, particularly in this room. And I have my friends surrounding me, my books, you see. The parishioners respect my time. Often I bring my old setter, Skye, with me. He's my only family now."

"We'd love to meet Skye; the two of us are dog lovers. I'm partial to Scottish Terriers myself. I can't speak for the doctor. We've met your unofficial helpers, but do you have an assistant to help you with day-to-day church business? A curate, perhaps?"

"A curate, indeed. That would be Mr. Blakely. Stewart Blakely. New to the job and I sent him to Swaffham on an errand. Deliberately, I may add. Didn't want to involve him in this investigation— yet."

"We'll have to interview Mr. Blakely as part of this investigation. Do you feel he is part of the problem?"

"No, no, I didn't mean to imply that. Blakely is, well, a bit different. Spent the past two years in New Guinea among indigenous folk. As you might suspect, getting him to relate to East Plumley has been a challenge. Nice enough lad, just can't seem to get inside his head. I'll be interested in what you have to think about him. More sherry, ladies?" Rose and Amaryllis shook their heads at the offer, but each did reach for one more shortbread.

Amaryllis brushed a crumb from her fingers and asked, "Have the constables any thoughts about the thefts?"

"None of the thefts has been reported to the police. Except the millstone. That sits, or sat, in a public place. The other two incidents were at private homes and the owners don't want curiosity seekers coming 'round. Can you blame them? And I have not reported the missing headstones for fear of raising alarms. I admit I've become a bit nervous about strolling the grounds for fear I'll discover more skullduggery. I'm not sure you are aware of East Plumley's limitations. Due to size, that is. We are too small to have a constable on site. We depend on Swaffham. They are top drawer when it comes to responding to our calls." The vicar looked contemplative and sad, templing his fingers and nodding at the fire.

"This is mischief of the first order, vicar, and I can tell you we'll find the thief or thieves. As I said earlier, Rose is my assistant. The two of us mean business. First, let me reassure you. The amount of lichen you have lost is considerable judging from what I have seen on the other stones. Considerable, but not enough to upset the balance of natural components in the churchyard, which is what I originally feared. A purveyor of antiques would hardly be interested in, as you put it, 'cheap concrete items' or crumbling headstones. Something else is driving this crime. Someone very cunning, and very smart, is risking a great deal to commit these thefts. And I suspect, for a significant sum of money. We *will* find out the what and the why of this operation that has brought us to East Plumley."

As they left St. Michael's, The visibly relaxed Reverend Coulton Ellington said, "I feel immensely better already. Having not one but two church ladies to ferret out the crime is the answer to my heartfelt prayer to the Almighty. Now, may I invite you both to be my guests at East Plumley's pub for a light supper? In England, of course, we call it 'tea' but I assure you that it will be a satisfying evening meal. Perhaps not gourmet, but most certainly will keep body and soul together."

"We'd be delighted, vicar. Rose has been absolutely smitten with that pub since she spotted it as we drove in. And how perfectly natural for the vicar to entertain his church survey team. Ready, Rose?"

Reverend Ellington shepherded his two guests along the High until they stood before the Rose and Thistle.

"A small lecture, if I may, ladies. I promise it will not take long." He smiled. "You are standing before East Plumley's oldest building; oldest on record, that is."

"What year are we talking about Vicar?"

"Closest guess, 1787 or '88. Josiah Benham staked out this land in 1785, and probably stuck around to see his legacy built sometime after that."

"Not to steal your thunder, Vicar, but I had a minute to read the brochures at the Arms. Most interesting, but tell us, who is the present owner?"

Rose could see Amaryllis fuming as she questioned the vicar. *Sorry good doctor, the vicar is not your sole property. He invited both of us to dinner and I intend to carry my end of the conversation.*

"Ah Mrs. McNess, thank you! You've just been spared my long and boring spiel! The present owner is Willis Mumford, who has just recently made a few controversial changes to the Rose."

"How so?" asked Amaryllis.

"New long mirror over the bar. Willis insisted that he wanted folks to see him as they entered and he could see them. His way of keeping an eye on the clientele."

"Perfectly rational idea," agreed Amaryllis.

"I agree. But after 200 years, *any* change seems controversial in a village of this size. By now folks have more or less accepted the mirror, and the brochures, and the half dozen new tables Willis added. Old 'Rose' sees far more business than before, and I credit Willis for that success."

"And his profits," chimed in Rose.

The trio laughed and the Vicar held the blue door as they preceded him into the Rose and Thistle.

෴

Chapter Eight

The Rose and Thistle bustled with activity as Reverend Ellington followed his two guests through the weathered blue door. The five o'clock crowd was boisterous. Heads swiveled to stare at the trio as they eased their way to a corner booth near the fireplace. Quizzical expressions quickly turned to smiles as the vicar was recognized.

But who were these two women? News of the 'church ladies' had not reached all ears in East Plumley. The vicar had never mentioned any relatives living nearby. Neither woman wore a clerical collar. Curious, indeed. Tongues wagged surreptitiously over the pints and shepherd's pies.

"Will this corner be satisfactory, ladies?"

"Perfect, vicar," said Amaryllis as she and Rose slid into the booth. Amaryllis was quick to give Rose the outer seat in hopes that her friend might pick up scraps of news. The fact that Amaryllis sat opposite the vicar and had his ear did not go unnoticed by Rose, who sat quietly and smiled her best 'church lady' smile.

"I can recommend The Rose's ale, and they have a certain bitter that I prefer. Their ciders are tops, as are their Pimm's. It's been a long day for each of us so I suggest we start with drink orders before we order our foodstuff. What will it be, ladies?"

"A glass of cider for me, please. Pear cider, if they have it. I'm partial to pear," said Rose.

"I'll have the same," added Amaryllis.

"Good choices, Mrs. McNess, Dr. Keynes-Livingston."

"Please, vicar! It's Rose and Frances!"

"At St. Michael's, perhaps, but here in the pub, *especially* in the pub, it would be unseemly for me—"

"NOO! You cannot make me! Hands off me! NO!"

CRASH!

"Ya crumb! Lego me arm!"

BOOM!

Ear-splitting sounds interrupted the vicar's words as pieces of crockery hit the floor next to their booth. The vicar raced to a table in the center of the pub and was clearly visible among the five or six other patrons crowded around the fracas.

Rose and Amaryllis froze in their seats. They watched in disbelief as the ruckus escalated into a full-blown fist fight between two individuals bent on destroying each other, plus a goodly amount of The Rose's crockery.

"Rose, you've got the front seat: can you see what's happening?"

"There are so many customers around the table it's hard to tell, but our vicar is in the thick of it. Wait! There's a tangle of bodies on the floor, including the vicar! Oh, I think he just took a hit on his chin!"

"Who?"

'The vicar! Reverend Ellington! For heaven's sake, Amaryllis, take your hands away from your eyes and *look!*"

"That's all we need! Missing gravestones and a wounded vicar!"

"Stop the drama, Amaryllis. This is a fist fight, not a shoot-out. Now. Wait: good!"

"What's good?"

"The vicar is escorting one of the parties to the back of The Rose. And the other fellow is leaving, too. Only he's going out The Rose's *front* door. Victor's choice? Whew! Floor show is over!"

"One can only hope that the vicar has had some influence on the perpetrators of this brawl. I'm sure we'll hear when he returns. *If* he returns—"

"Deebs, here! Vicar sent me to take drink orders as he'll be delayed a bit. What is your fancy, ladies?"

"Deebs? Is everything settled? Or should I say, quiet for the moment? Is the vicar all right?"

"Right as rain, Ma'am. Took a nasty knock on his chin when 'Trouble' tried to get away from 'im. But vicar's not a 'bleeder': he'll be fine. Too bad you had to see a dust-up; dinn'it happen often. 'Specially with a reg'lar. Drinks, ladies?"

A subdued Amaryllis ordered pear cider for the two of them and watched the lanky, smiling Deebs disappear toward the bar.

"I would call that 'information overload', wouldn't you, Amaryllis? At least he didn't laugh at your questions. Deebs. Curious name. Easy to remember that one," smiled Rose.

The two church ladies sipped their cider and studied the dark-framed sepia photographs on the walls until Reverend Ellington returned to the booth. He was adjusting his clerical collar in one hand and smoothing his hair with the other. The large square of sticking plaster on his left jaw gave him the appearance of an over-aged wrangler returning from his last round-up. Rugged masculinity was not lost on his guests.

"Sorry, ladies. I know that sounds frightfully lame. I *sincerely* regret that an incident like this is your introduction to The Rose. We don't see this often, I promise. But when a ruckus breaks out—"

"You had to go!" whispered Amaryllis. "Rose and I certainly understand. Are you all right? You will share the *raison d'être* with us, I hope."

"Of course, of course, and I'm fine; it's just a nick. Couldn't have been a more public stage for a show of pugnacity, could it? Let's wait until we get our meals: I've ordered shepherd's pie for all. Hope that's all right with you ladies. It is definitely the pub's specialty."

"Ah, Deebs! My bitter! A most welcome refreshment at the moment."

"And pies'll be out in a moment; cook's just put 'em on the hob right now."

"Ladies, you are about to partake of a little bit of English heaven. I'd wager a healthy tithe on the goodness of this meal. God Bless."

"Before that young man returns, vicar, could you clarify his name for me: is it really 'Deebs'?"

Reverend Ellington leaned back and smiled. "Yes, Mrs. McNess, it really is. That's all he's called and he is a mainstay of this pub. His last name? If I've ever known, I've long forgotten. But you'll never forget young Deebs! Ah, I believe our supper is on its way!" The three tucked into their steaming shepherd's pies, ordered more cider, and thoroughly enjoyed the convivial atmosphere of The Rose and Thistle.

Rose took advantage of her outside seat and was engrossed with the constant hum of activity around her. So much to see. Those old football pennants tell a lot of history. This was a smart move on the vicar's part, introducing us to the pub. Certainly I'll try to get back here tomorrow. Maybe I can make myself look a bit more familiar to the regulars, sit closer to the bar in order to chat a bit and pick up a few secrets. And listen. Someone in this village knows a thing or two about the hijinks that are going on at St. Michael's.

Interruptions by three or four townspeople were received jovially as the vicar eagerly introduced his guests in the most innocent of terms. He was firm in his intent to keep any whisper of church investigation silent. At least as long as possible.

"Church surveys you say?" asked Mr. James Willoughby, whom the vicar described as "one of my stalwarts at St. Michael's, and also a fair golfing partner."

"What sort of surveys do they want now? Didn't we have a committee doing that last year, Coulton?"

"Ah, I believe this is one concerning OAP's roles in churchyard accessibility," replied the Vicar.

"You handled that well," whispered Rose as Mr. Willoughby strode away.

"Coulton, my man!" boomed their next visitor. "Where have you been keeping these lovely ladies?" The vicar smiled, stood and introduced the two women.

"Mrs. McNess is from Virginia and Dr. Keynes-Livingston has just joined us from a stay in Australia. They will be conducting a church survey at St. Michael's for a few days. Part of a worldwide undertaking. Ladies, may I present my friend, Rupert Pennington. Rupert has served twice as my senior warden and has been town solicitor for over thirteen years."

"My pleasure, ladies, to meet you both. Sit down, Coulton, I didn't mean to interrupt your tea. Any more than it has been interrupted. Hope your chin won't hamper your sermon on Sunday, my friend. Nice job you did with young Botts, vicar. Shouldn't be seeing him back here anytime soon. Is he still helping old Willem?"

"Yes, vestry agreed on six months. I've heard no complaints so far."

"Well, Coulton, I trust your excellent judgment. You know I always have. Good night, ladies; I hope your stay in our little village is most pleasant!" Giving the trio a jaunty salute, Rupert Pennington smoothed a tan cap onto his head and exited The Rose.

What a supercilious man. You'd think he was a cabinet member by the way he puffed himself up. Glad the vicar doesn't have him as a golfing partner. Or does he? Rose put these thoughts aside and turned to the vicar with, "I am about to pop with curiosity. Is it a good time to tell us what happened earlier? Deebs called it a 'dust up'!"

"Hardly! It is unfortunate, and sadly, it does involve St. Michael's indirectly." Both women were wide-eyed at this revelation.

"You recall meeting Willem Botts this afternoon? Our sexton, caretaker, man of all works at St. Michael's for over three decades! Willem is guardian for his nephew, Trevor Botts. Parents died in an accident when Trevor was an infant, and Willem is his only kin. He's done an admirable job, rather *tried* to do so. Trevor refuses his, or any one's help. Left school in sixth form, drifted from place to place in East Plumley and beyond."

"You mean homeless?" asked Rose.

"Almost. He would find a family to take him in for a while. After he'd commit another awful misdemeanor, they'd kick him out and he'd move on. A rolling stone, going from bad to worse. Then he finally returned to Willem's door. And Willem took him on as 'assistant' at St. Michael's, to do menial chores in the churchyard, sweeping the hallways, emptying trash on Monday mornings."

"How long has he been working at St. Michael's?"

"Let's see. I talked it over with the vestry when Willem proposed this to me. The vestry agreed Botts could try this arrangement for six months. It started in December, so he's been with us nearly four months."

"How did the fight break out?" Rose asked.

"This afternoon Trevor's pitiful sidekick stood him the price of two ales, but refused, or did not have the money, for another. Trevor started scrapping with his friend and Willis, the pub's owner, for a third. Willis and I got Trevor out the back door and handed him a large coffee. Trevor would have been charged with drunk and disorderly conduct if there had been any constables nearby. The sidekick's the fellow you may have seen slinking out the front door."

"Do you have a drug problem in East Plumley? Or rather, do you suspect Trevor of having a drug problem, vicar?" asked Rose.

"Certainly there are a few teens who experiment, Mrs. Mc-Ness, but not so I would call it 'rampant'. Trevor could be suspect, but he has little or no money. Nor any friends from whom to beg or borrow, or steal."

"Reverend Ellington, I am asking these questions as a curious old lady. But *also* as a curious old lady here to find out what is happening in your churchyard. I do not know how my friend Amaryllis feels, but right now I think you have just handed us a 'person of interest' in the case of the missing tombstones!"

Chapter Nine

After "Goodnight!" and "Do come back!" from their new acquaintances, Rose and Amaryllis walked the short distance back to the Arms and collapsed wearily onto their sofas.

"How could we forget that when the Brits say 'tea', it is a full-blown lunch? Or in our case, dinner. I'm so full that I don't think I can make it to bed."

"Not so full that a dram of brandy wouldn't go down easily. How about it, Rose? To close the door on a long and, I must say, satisfying day."

"You're going to be a bad influence, Amaryllis. But . . . why not? Just a wee dram though."

"We need this to sort out our thoughts. Would you look at this lovely amber color? My, the English do know how to make one feel welcome."

"Agreed. But tell me, aside from the brandy, how do you think our introduction went?"

"Swimmingly, Rose. The vicar is quite 'dishy'. Especially with his bandaged jaw. And assuredly intelligent. He's obviously worried sick about resolving this caper. Rather, *crime*. It won't affect his position in the church, but it is damaging church property, and also some of the town's. I must take samples of the lichen from the remaining concrete headstones. I'll do that tomorrow. This mischief is spreading and must be stopped."

"You give me the shivers, Amaryllis, but I agree with everything you say. I'll get busy with my snooping while you carry out your scientific investigations. As to Coulton Ellington being, how did you describe him, 'dishy'? Don't you get any ideas."

"Now come, Rose, wouldn't you at least agree he's very attractive? And you are quite the eligible widow . . . about his age I would say. You know what we discussed about attention from the opposite sex—"

"Amaryllis! No more! I have just one more thought for the evening before I fall asleep on the spot."

"And that is?"

"I want to find out more about young Botts and this Blakely fellow. Blakely sounds a bit wobbly to me. I couldn't tell if the vicar didn't trust him or didn't care for him."

"Rose, you are, and please do not be offended at this, akin to a dog with a bone! You will certainly worry the truth out. I *knew* I *had* the perfect partner."

After a quick hug the two friends retired to their respective rooms and closed their doors firmly behind them.

Chapter Ten

Sleep did not come for Rose. After an hour or two twisting and turning on the unfamiliar bed, Rose pushed aside the heavy duvet and curled up in the lounge chair by the window. I'm tired as the mischief but somehow too tired to sleep. What is it? I've got this notion that just won't leave my head. Annie would say 'Oh, Mom, not one of your notions again!' But she's learned that my notions are almost always right! 'Spot on!' as the Brits would say. I've got this feeling about Amaryllis. And the vicar. She's very vulnerable right now. And basically, lonely, despite the bravado she spouts. She can run circles around me academically but sometimes 'smarts' can ignore the emotions. She's not mentioned her children but that's no surprise. They are all older and no doubt accustomed to their mother's escapades. Amaryllis is alone in this wide, wide world. I suspect that she and the Vicar have more in common than the desire to solve this mystery. She was terribly abrupt with him tonight . . . but I don't think she meant to be. Nervousness? Perhaps. I'm the one to be nervous if she's put me in charge of solving this mystery. I'll just have to wait and see if this notion persists. I wonder how the vicar feels about Amaryllis . . .if he consideres her 'dishy'.

ꝏꙨꙩꙫ

The Reverend Coulton Simon Ellington bade his guests good-night, watched as they navigated the uneven sidewalk until they reached The Plumley Arms, then turned to walk to the dark and silent rectory. Of course, he could have driven to The Rose this evening, but the ladies had experienced a full day of driving and seemed eager for the walk. Besides, it wasn't that far and it seemed silly to go back to the. rectory to fetch his car, drive the short distance to the pub, find a parking spot, then retrace the trip after two ales. No, the walk would clear his mind. And the cool air might ease the ache in his jaw.

Damn if that wasn't a punch young Trevor landed! A few inches to the right and I would have lost the new crown Dr. Simms just put in place.

Certainly wasn't prepared for Dr. Keynes-Livingston. Mrs. McNess seems genuinely interested in our little village. A rather gentle soul. Refined, quiet. But there is a sparkle in her eye! Dr. Keynes-Livingston is not what I'd call your typical scientist. But then old Thailman warned me about her. Rather, he predicted she would get to the heart of the matter expeditiously. And with little or no fanfare. A no-nonsense sort of a woman. Perhaps a bit aloof, but rather comely, I do say. I'm sure there are curves beneath that severe jacket she was wearing. Didn't Thailman mention she'd just come off a divorce?

Coulton, don't even go there! This situation is messy enough without letting personal feelings surface. We've got to find out what's going on in our churchyard. Could ordinary lichen be the reason for the thefts? Of course, the doctor doesn't think any lichen is ordinary…but lichen that has been growing quietly here for centuries? Congregation was grumbling about the loss of three gravestones last month; what will they say at our next meeting? Whoa! Here I am: easy walk. Not even half-past. Time to take old Skye for his evening constitutional.

Reverend Ellington turned the key in the vicarage door and was met by the thump-thump of the aging setter's tail against the parlor rug.

"Skye, old fellow! Off the rug! Let's us two gents have a good short walk!"

Chapter Eleven

Rose stretched, hugged the plump pillow and gathered the duvet around her shoulders. I should get up. I should get up. I *should* get up. Why does it get harder and harder to rouse myself in the morning? This bed is so comfy that I, well, I just do not want to face the unpleasant situation that we may be facing. That is the real truth of the matter. Get up, Rose McNess, get up. Nothing can be so awful if the sliver of daylight coming through those heavy draperies is . . . sunshine. Yes! Hooray! Probably a spot of rain any minute but at this instant . . . sun.

Cheered at the prospect of another sunny morning, Rose climbed out of bed and completed her morning ablutions quickly. Traveling with one piece of luggage certainly keeps one's wardrobe decisions simple. I'll wear my tweeds and twin-set. It will be a perfect day for exploring East Plumley. Just exploring, no sleuthing. A sturdy shoes sort of day. Why was I so timid about getting out of bed?

Buoyed, Rose opened the door to greet Amaryllis. The good doctor was reclining lazily among the plump cushions on the sofa as she sipped her morning cup of tea.

"My word, Rose, aren't you looking perky this morning?"

"Please, Amaryllis, *not* perky."

"Touchy this morning, are we?"

"Not touchy, Amaryllis. I detest being described as 'perky'. Sparrows are perky. Jack Russell terriers are perky. Zinnias are perky. Little old ladies are not perky."

"Sorry, dear. Could I describe you, then, as 'determined'? Your attire, your demeanor, your firm chin thrust forward: all convey determination. What *are* you up to today?"

"'Determined' I will accept. As for today: first I shall partake of a large bowl of porridge, one or more scones with my coffee, and then I shall merely stroll through East Plumley."

"Following the trail of the missing pieces the vicar described?"

"That is not in my plan for today. Or at least this morning. I want to see how East Plumley lives. I'll visit some of the shops, chat with the owners and perhaps a customer or two. I'll explore what interests me and generally get acquainted with the town. Think of it as slipping into a pair of favorite slippers, Amaryllis: I want to feel comfortable in East Plumley."

"Bravo, Rose. Once again, I'll say it: I picked the perfect partner for this adventure. Off you go. I'm giving myself a lie-in before I take off to St. Michael's for more digging and scraping."

❦

Amaryllis straightened herself in the bed until she was sitting upright. Three clouds of feathery pillows propped her back and the silky, smooth duvet tickled her chin.

I certainly hit a nerve with dear Rose. But dammit, she did look perky. And unless I am too far behind the times, that is not an insult. She has always been so proper and forthright. I really thought I was complimenting her. I almost wish I could shadow her as she goes all over East Plumley finding folks to talk to, looking for clues to this damnable mystery. Why, back at Wynfield Farms, Rose would engage the even the shy ones and get them to talk. She would chat them up a bit and then get each and every person to do her bidding. Willingly and with a smile.

But I just can't fathom how she will start a conversation about the missing gravestones, "I say, did you happen to pick up a gravestone from St. Michael's?" Or, "Have you seen any-one carrying a large parcel from the churchyard?"

Really. No, I cannot see Rose being that direct. Or stupid. She'll probably start a conversation about the weather. It is rather brilliant and blue today. Or flowers: she loves flowers and there are loads of gardens here to inspect and chat about. And animals. A pity she hasn't found a terrier here. Particularly a Scottie. Now that would set her off! But as we learned the first evening, there are a zillion cats in East Plumley. Rose could start knocking on doors to try to locate homes for the pitiful beasts. Then she'd have her foot over the doorstep and a real inside look into some of the homes. But I am simply being fanciful and indulging myself because I am feeling guilty for upsetting Rose.

I recognize that I am not especially good with people. Empathetic: that's the word. I have little empathy. Or warmth. That's the word Winslow used. "Amaryllis, you have no warmth." Well, he certainly didn't complain in the bedroom. Scientists do not need warmth. Give me a spotless laboratory, a microscope and a challenge.

I should remind myself that I have the luxury of dealing with cold, impersonal slides with yummy unidentified lichen that could hold the key to this mystery. Lichen that I have never encountered before. Lichen that I do not have to be nice to, apologize to, or even say goodbye to at the end of the day. Indeed, I think my job is the easier one in East Plumley. Was I not smart in putting Rose in charge?

I must say the vicar seems terribly pleasant. And respectful. I <u>do</u> like that in a man. No, <u>like</u> is not the right word: I demand respect from a man. Particularly one with whom I shall be in close contact for many hours a day. Yes, Reverend Ellington, we'll get along just fine.

With that change of head and heart, Amaryllis threw back the duvet, swung her long legs out of bed, and prepared to meet the day in East Plumley. In her own way.

Chapter Twelve

Rose McNess enjoyed her solitary breakfast in the Arms' gracious dining salon. As she sipped the last of her coffee she asked herself why Amaryllis' remarks rankled.

If she hadn't been lolling there in the cushions a la 'Queen of the May' I guess it wouldn't have sounded so offensive. I know she didn't mean to be critical but it just struck me that way. I cannot afford to be too sensitive: it is Amaryllis' show. She's the expert here and I'm the tag-along. Pray I remember that.

Rose finished her last sip of coffee, patted her mouth with her napkin and placed the folded cloth beside her plate.

I probably should go back upstairs and say goodbye to Amaryllis but that would look as if I were apologizing and why should I apologize? Rose McNess, get over it and get moving.

Rose stood in front of The Plumley Arms and looked to her left. She could see a number of people moving in and out of the High Street shops, probably as delighted with the fair weather as she.

And here I thought I was an early bird! No such thing on a fine day I suppose. Rose crossed the High and turned toward Bibbs' Green Grocer. As she entered under the green-as-grass awning she was startled by a voice at her elbow,

'Allo, Missus, come for my fresh peas this morning?"

Startled, Rose laughed and said, "No, but I would surely take a sample if you are passing them out."

"Oooh, yer a visitor from the States, eh? Welcome to Bibbs', finest greens and sundry in East Plumley!"

"And you are, sir?" asked Rose, as demurely as she could manage.

"Meekins' me name. Wilford Meekins, Sr. That's Junior, back in storage. 'Ere's the peas. Ever see such?"

Rose reached into the brown parchment bag Meekins was holding, picked out one plump green pea and popped it into her mouth.

"How 's it? Full of sugar 'tis."

"Delicious, Mr. Meekins. Simply delicious. I'd always sneak a raw pea or two when I was shelling them for supper. But these are so early. In the States we never had fresh peas until late April, or mid-May."

"These beauties are from the south. They get more sun, milder winters, than 'ere in East Plumley."

"Has Bibbs' been in business for years and years? Bringing folks greens and goods from all over?" Rose had been looking at the bins full of oranges and lemons from Spain, melons from Israel, rutabagas and cabbages from Germany.

"Walter Bibbs opened 'is doors in 1895 and never missed a day until he died in 1933. Me father took over until he died in 1955, and then 'twas my turn. Junior, he'll be next unless he gets other ideas."

"If have any questions about East Plumley, I'll know just where to come for answers. I would bet that you know your town inside and out, Mr. Meekins." Rose said this with a smile as she helped herself to another plump green pea. "I should pay you for the produce I've consumed and be on my way."

Wilford Meekins roared and shook his head. "No Missus, please. A pleasure to meet an American who knows good produce. And eats it like a lady."

"I thank you for the compliment, Mr. Meekins. Since I am new to East Plumley and want to explore everything along the High, where would you suggest I go next?"

Meekins' expression turned thoughtful as he pondered Rose's question. "T'wouldn't want you botherin' next door. Shady business, that."

"Oh? Hard to believe 'shady business' in this lovely village."

"Yer don'no Celeste. Calls 'erself 'Alterations'. It's what she alters that's shady."

"You sound quite mysterious Mr. Meekins. Am I to guess she, uh, changes peoples' lives as well as their garments?"

"Might do. Tried to change the vicar, din't she?"

"Oh, my word. I've met Reverend Ellington and am very impressed by the man."

"So was Celeste!" roared Mr. Meekins. "She set 'er cap for that man soon as she learned his wife passed. Fancied up to 'im, caterin' tea parties for the fellow. Hummph. Few of the lads had a word with vicar and that stopped Celeste. Oh, she still does a load of business but not with the vicar. For sure not the vicar!"

"Forewarned is forearmed, Mr. Meekins. Again, I thank you for your hospitality."

"And do no' pass AGELESS: that's where the old stuff stays. Pop in and see Miss Tilly. Tell her Meekins sent you."

ᘓᗥᘐ

So, AGELESS it is. I do love antique shops so that will be a joy . . . unless . . . Here! Right in the shadow of Bibbs'. Is that the mysterious Celeste, sitting in the doorway?

Rose had ventured a few steps from the green grocers when she glanced to her left and saw an attractive brunette sitting on a folding chair in the dark and narrow doorway. The neatly lettered sign above advertised simply, 'ALTERATIONS.'.

"Pardon, but would you be Celeste?"

The woman laughed, a deep, musical laugh, and looked up at Rose with a wide smile. She was wearing a silky, black kimono in a print of magenta and coral that, upon closer inspection (which Rose was now enjoying) proved itself to be a floral of intricate design. Rose saw that it loosely covered an ample bosom and immediately understood why the men of East Plumley were smitten. And why they were happy to bring their alterations to Celeste.

"I would be, and am, the one and only Celeste in East Plumley. I see you are coming from Bibbs' and no doubt 'Mistaken Meekins' has told you all about me. Come in, come in, and have a cup of tea. I assure you I am harmless."

Rose laughed and found herself unable to refuse Celeste's offer. "A cuppa would be delightful. I cannot linger, nor refuse an invitation, especially one so freely offered. Thank you."

Celeste rose. Kimono trailing, she tucked her chair under one arm, led Rose through a narrow entranceway and held the door as she ushered her guest into the tiny atelier.

"What a stunning place! I am enchanted!"

"My shoebox, I call it. Small though it is, I love it."

"Compact, Celeste, compact and neat. At our age, do we need acres of room? Why, my home is just about the same size."

"And may I inquire, where is your home?"

"I do apologize, Celeste. I'm Rose McNess, from the state of Virginia in the United States. And my home is in a, well, I guess you would call it a 'senior village'. We call it a retirement home."

"And are you all alone there?"

"If you mean am I *single*? Yes, I have been widowed twice. And I live among many others but we all have our separate, well, flats. I'm never really alone, unless I chose to be. As I said, my condo is just about the size of your shoebox."

"I feel as if had stepped down the rabbit hole into Alice's wonderland. This is an artist's paradise. Celeste— if I may call you that— this place is delightful. And do you actually work on your alterations in this enchanting room?"

"Absolutely. You are standing in front of my trusted machine. Very old but very faithful . . . not unlike some of my friends! Of course, much of my work is done by hand."

"But these paintings, your collection of Wedgwood, your Meissen, all of your fabrics . . . they show that you have a real *gift*. An artist's eye . . . and soul."

Rose stared at the vibrant medley of stripes, dots, fringes, all in hot, primary colors that blended to bring light and gaiety to the narrow room. Near the room's one undersized window there was a chaise, its coverlet of turquoise almost obscured by a phalanx of gaily covered pillows and a sleeping tabby. Rose couldn't help but wonder why the cat wasn't dressed in gay colors to match the rest of the room.

"I cannot tell you how lovely it is to be appreciated. Thank you for your kind words. I feel we are kindred spirits."

"I have to admit, Celeste, I appreciate art and fine fabrics." Rose paused and continued, "Mr. Meekins doesn't appear to be your biggest fan. He mentioned something about the vicar…"

Celeste roared, her deep musical laugh filling the tiny room. "I assure you I did have an eye for Coulton. When his wife passed, he was bereft. The man was lonely. He needed some femininity in his barren life. He needed . . . sex."

Rose gulped, looked wide-eyed at Celeste and willed her to continue.

"Not to worry; the vicar was too proper. I did provide a shoulder for him to lean upon and let him shed a tear or two, but that was it. Poor old Meekins; got his knickers in a twist just thinking about it. No, Celeste did not corrupt the vicar . . . though she wanted to!"

"A widower may often find himself desperately lonely, especially if he's had a long and happy marriage," mused Rose.

"Oh, Vicar weren't lonely for long! All the East Plumley ladies beat a path to his door. When they realized he was more interested in Skye, his old setter, than in 'feminine companionship', his meal plan dwindled like snow in June. That's when he'd come to see Celeste: Vicar and Skye! Oh, we would have some grand chats over our sherries."

Her hostess turned and somehow produced two cups of steaming tea from a small trolley hidden behind an exotic oriental screen. Rose accepted the proffered cup and asked, "And…do you frequent St. Michael's? For church services and the like?"

"Absolutely. You'll find me in the second row on the right every Sunday. The vicar and I usually share a wink or two. And occasionally a sherry on Thursdays. He's a good man, Coulton is."

"Oh, I agree. A very good man. Celeste, this is delightful. I have a lot of East Plumley to cover today. Thank you for sharing your studio, and your thoughts and tea. I do look forward to seeing you again. If not at St. Michael's—"

"Perhaps you'll come back? I hope so. You have given me a lift this morning."

They returned to the High through the narrow pass-through and Celeste waved Rose on her way.

Rose thought this was one experience Amaryllis would have enjoyed. *Golly*. Celeste is her sort of woman. I dare say there are not many 'Celeste's' in East Plumley. Or am I being naïve?

Chapter Thirteen

A shoe repair shop, buffeted on one side by a small jewelry store and a ladies' ready to wear on the other, caught Rose's eye but not her interest. She spotted AGELESS a few doors along and hurried for fear it might close for lunch hour.

How could it be almost noon already? I haven't covered half of what I set out to explore. And it does look more and more like rain is coming.

AGELESS was housed in a fragile stone cottage that boasted two useless dormers on its shingled roof, an enormous bow window across its front, and a wooden door that appeared as wide as it was tall. A small window to the right of the door was losing purchase to the ivy creeping across the front. Greenery had not, however, obscured the fine lettering on the sign that swung over the entrance: AGELESS ANTIQUES-Yours Forever.

Rose pushed gently and the massive door creaked open a

few inches. She pushed again and entered the dimly lit world of the past.

"May I help you?"

Rose blinked, and looked around, hoping to put sight to sound.

"Over here, dearie. Just beyond the Irish rocking horse."

Rose could barely discern a shape in a far corner, obscured, as she had just been informed, by a majestic wooden horse, replete with arched neck and flowing mane.

"Miss Tilly?"

"Indeed! Old Meekins must have sent you to me! He's the only one I allow to call me 'Miss Tilly'."

"Oh, sorry, I just thought—"

"No, dearie, Miss Tilly will do. You're American? Are you looking for something special to take home?"

"Just memories, Miss Tilly. May I introduce myself? I'm Rose, Mrs. Rose McNess, and I'm here with a friend to do a survey on churches in the region. We're visiting St. Michael's, of course. And staying at The Arms. This morning I'm trying to get acquainted with East Plumley, and your place is one I could hardly wait to visit."

Miss Tilly emerged from the shadows of the Irish rocking horse, the grandfather's clock, and dozens of Staffordshire dogs. She was a tiny woman, barely five feet, with a face as wrinkled and brown as an apple put up for winter storage. Her sparse hair, a vibrant henna, contrasted with the clear blue of her deep-set eyes. She had the look of a person who does not miss a moment in this world.

"Oh, I've heard about your coming to East Plumley. Of course it's all about the mysterious goings-on at St. Michael's. I don't get around much these days, but news does filter in to Miss Tilly."

"You've hit a nerve, Miss Tilly, and the truth for our visit. I won't try to fool you with our "survey" ruse. And since you've guessed, can you shed any light on the matter? Who would dig up and carry away old gravestones?"

"Whoever it is, has to be pretty stupid. They'd have to know they would be found out, sooner or later. Right now I can't think of anyone in East Plumley who's that dumb. I sell a few items to locals, but mostly I meet visitors, or tourists going on to Swaffham. No idiots, that's what I'm saying."

"Are there any real 'characters' living around here? Anyone you can think of?"

"All the 'characters', as you call them, are my age! And pretty damn smart! Can you imagine an eighty-five-year-old man carrying away a gravestone?"

"You're NOT eighty-five!"

"Yes, dearie, this past February. And I don't plan on going anywhere soon."

"This has been a delight, meeting you. You're, you're an

inspiration. I'll be right up there with you in a few years. None of us are youngsters any—"

"Wait! I said I didn't know any 'characters'. I do. Not really *know* the lad but know of him. Pitiful situation. Knew his Mam and Pap well; good people. Lad's name's Trevor. Trevor Botts. Last I heard he's living with his uncle. Mind you, that's hear-say, but I get pretty good hear-say in AGELESS. That Trevor might not be stupid, but I do know he's needy. In every way, *needy.* "

"Miss Tilly, thank you so much. That's information I'll tuck away. Oh, I wish I could take home a truckload of your wonderful antiques. But I cannot. And at my age, I'm trying to shed, not add. Goodbye, and thank you for your time. And your wisdom."

"Goodbye, dearie. I hope I'll see you again. Probably at St. Michael's."

Rose left the cluttered shop as the town clock was striking twelve.

Noon already. Golly, I didn't cover all the shops on the High but I surely made a dent in the number. And what characters. It is almost tempting to want to stay on and become a part of the life here. Rose, Rose: don't be silly. You are meeting David in London when this caper is behind us and then back to Wynfield Farms. Enough daydreaming.

Trevor. Surely I'll remember that little nugget.

Smiling to herself and humming a nameless tune, Rose crossed the High and returned to the Plumley Arms.

Chapter Fourteen

The morning had been almost perfect. Weather fine, the characters encountered delightful, and how glad she was that she'd worn her most comfortable shoes. It wasn't walking but standing about that gave her legs an occasional ache. Noon already: lunch time or tea time? I'll go to the suite, freshen up and then decide: stay in or try one of the little tea shops down the way.

Giles greeted Rose as she entered the Arms.

"Good morning, Madam, or should I say, good afternoon? Quarter past already. The good doctor has already picked up the key, Mrs. McNess. I believe you shall find her in the suite."

"Thank you, Giles. I'm on my way."

So Amaryllis is already back from St. Michael's. Wonder if she uncovered anything of interest this morning? Or if she and the Vicar proved to be compatible in their work? I'll suggest we lunch together. If she calls me 'perky', forget it! But I am dying to tell her about the characters I met!

"Amaryllis, back already? Anything new at St. Michael's?"

"Not in two hundred years, Rose, if you don't count that awful tacked-on porch! How was your exploring, dear?"

"Absolutely marvelous! May I suggest we find a quiet tea room for a sandwich and let me tell you all about it?"

Peace! Rose smiled her brightest smile at her roommate and the morning was forgiven. *Somehow, I think Amaryllis and the Vicar were compatible today.*

"I'd love that!"

"Let me freshen up and hit the High. The weather has changed— time for our raincoats."

ⱷⱺⱺ

Ten minutes later the two ladies dropped their keys into Giles' waiting hand and started down East Plumley's thoroughfare in search of the perfect tea shop.

"How about this one, Rose? Was it on your list this morning?"

"Sunshine's Sandies. I'm assuming a 'sandy' means sandwich. Let's try it, Amaryllis: Sunshine's because it's raining outside."

The pair entered and found an empty table near the back corner. "Just made for us, Amaryllis. I can't believe I didn't see this place today, but tucked around the corner it's easy to miss."

Sunshine's was decorated with beaming faces of the sun in every color and material: copper, bronze, tin, ceramic, pa-

pier-mâché and other elements impossible to decipher. Rose
and Amaryllis were so occupied with the decor that neither
of them noticed the plump blonde waitress standing by their
table. She finally spoke, in a broad accent that took some time
to fully understand. Smiles and a large menu helped ease their
order and soon chicken salad sandwiches and a pot of hot
tea appeared before them.

"Amaryllis, I think you've discovered a gem. Best chicken
salad I've had since Wynfield Farms!"

"I agree! But between bites, tell me about your morning.
You look as if you've had a marvelous adventure. I can tell
by the color in your cheeks."

"It *was* marvelous. Bibbs' is the place to shop for veggies; it's international. Produce from all over the world.
Not unusual, I suppose, but a wonder to see such items
here in March."

"But you didn't spend all your time among the veggies?"

"Heavens, no! I met the most intriguing woman, Amaryllis. Probably what the ladies of East Plumley call 'a lady of
the night'. But she's not! She just wants to give that impression. Or at least that's my opinion. And her atelier is unbe-
lievable. I guarantee there is no other place like it in this
village. All color and light and lovely paintings and…"

"Whoa! I'm intrigued. Where does this character reside?"

"That's the most remarkable thing. She lives in a long, narrow room that looks as if it once was part of the jewelry shop

next door. Smaller even than my condo at Wynfield farms. A tiny room, but, oh, so full of light and gaiety that I could have lingered all morning."

"Does this person have a name? I'm sure you introduced yourself—"

"Celeste. Her name is Celeste. I didn't even ask her last name; I couldn't have remembered anyway. She's from the Czech Republic. Her profession is alterations and a bit of hand-holding on the side. She attends St. Michael's; I'll introduce you if she's there on Sunday."

"Rose, trust you to find the town's characters! Were there others on your schedule this morning?"

"Ah, Miss Tilly of AGELESS ANTIQUES. Older, even, than I. But with the brightest henna rinse that you've ever seen. Perfectly delightful. And I did ask her if she knew of any 'characters' in the town."

"How did you put that, Rose? Delicately, I trust?"

"Absolutely. And guess what? She told me about Willem Botts' nephew: the one involved in the scrap at the pub. Miss Tilly had known his parents and repeated what the vicar told us about his homeless situation."

"Did you have to purchase something to get out of the antique store, Rose?"

"I was very strong, Amaryllis. Not one pence left my purse. However, I may return to purchase a charming tea caddy that was crying out, 'Buy me, buy me.'"

The two sleuths laughed and gossiped as they finished their lunch. When they stopped for breath, they were amazed to see that every table in the small shop was filled with hungry patrons.

"This is a popular place, Rose. Let's remember it. Neither of us needs the hearty luncheon that The Arms entices us to eat."

"I agree. And no dessert for me today. Tea times have helped the waistband shrink since we've been over here. Let's settle up and—"

Rose was interrupted by two women who approached their table.

"Good afternoon! We've heard of the survey team that has come to look at our St. Michael's and overhearing your accents, well, we put two and two together," solemnly spoke Ms. Tall Lady.

"We're long-time members of St. Michael's and just say we hope everything goes smoothly for you while you are among us," added Mrs. Long Face.

Amaryllis did the honors of their introductions.

"We're delighted to be a part of East Plumley. This is a lovely village, and you have a fine vicar. We are honored to be among you."

The foursome chatted pleasantly for a few more moments and then the Missus Tall Lady and Long Face waved good-bye, whispering, in parting, "Just don't take our vicar back to America with you!"

"Well," said Amaryllis, "that was certainly an unexpected gesture. The Brits are not ones to push themselves forward like that. Particularly the ladies. Tells you the sort of town this is, don't you agree?"

"I've gotten nothing but friendly greetings all morning," Rose replied. "But I also think those ladies just fired a warning shot across our bow."

"Whatever do you mean?"

"Don't take the vicar away. Plainly, every woman in the parish is in love with the man!"

Chapter Fifteen

Rose's persistent internal alarm jiggled at her usual waking hour: 6:20 A.M. She squirmed to extricate herself from the silky duvet and sat for a moment dangling her feet.

Whew! I've never slept as soundly. Have to get some feeling back in these old feet. Something tells me I'll be covering a lot of territory again today if I'm going to be of much help to Amaryllis. Wonder if she is up yet?

A call to her friend elicited no response. Rose saw that Amaryllis had left her bedroom door open and placed a large note on the table in their sitting room.

"OFF FOR COFFEE AND ST. MICHAEL'S. WILL TRY TO MEET YOU BACK HERE 3:00 P.M. YOU KNOW WHERE YOU CAN FIND ME."

That I do! Well, I better get moving. Why does it get harder and harder to get started in the morning? Coffee. That's what I need right now. Coffee and toast and I'll be ready to take on the world. Or at least, East Plumley.

Rose dressed quickly. Today is definitely another twin set and tweed outfit. Isn't that what every respectable early morning shopper wears? She scurried down the stairs, dropped her key at the desk, and left The Plumley Arms without being spotted or stopped by Giles.

That man is too conscientious! He should certainly know that two church ladies are not going to abscond with the key to his castle! Now, let me see: which of the tea shoppes looks more promising? Or more to the point, which is open at 7:00 *AM?* Rose crossed High Street and found that the door at Mary's Own was propped open with a large wooden ladle allowing a delightful aroma of cinnamon to waft onto the High. Rose tentatively poked her head inside and called, "Shall I close the door behind me?"

"No, no, Ma'am. All closed, m'windows get steamed and folks won't be able to see what's goin' on in here. Come in, Ma'am, come in! Yer the first of m'day. Sit down and I'll be over with coffee."

Rose smiled and chose a small table close to the large display case. The owner of the voice had yet to appear. Rose wondered if Mary's Own was really open for business.

Suddenly a small elfin figure sprang from behind the case and propelled herself toward Rose. Her jet-black hair was damp, with wispy tendrils framing her flushed face as if it were a cameo.

"Sorry! Steam's fierce in my baking room. M'best coffee, m'lady, and Mary's famous buns? One, or two?"

"Oh, my. Well, definitely two. If your buns are as divine as the aroma that led me inside, I may want three! Wait, are those scones? I'll have one of each please. Tell me, are you 'Mary'?"

Between chuckles Mary admitted that she was a 'Mary,' only the great-great-granddaughter of the original.

"'Bout you: from the States? Visitin' kin?"

"No, no kin. But yes, from the States. I'm here as part of a team making a church survey. We'll be looking at St. Michael's. We understand it is a lovely old church. In fact, my colleague is there now, looking at the churchyard."

"Hmmmph. Wouldn't think it wise to dawdle in the churchyard after the hijinks happened there."

"Why, what do you mean?" asked Rose, properly shocked.

"Some of them kids, prob'ly the technical kids. Made off with three headstones. Must've happened two, three, weeks ago. Devils they be! Taking some old folks stones to do what? Mischief. That's all." Warming to her story and noting that Rose was listening with rapt attention, Mary asked, "D'ye mind if have a sit-down for a sec? Been baking since 4:00 A.M. and m' knees can use a rest."

"Oh, please do, Mary. And tell me anything else you know about this crime. And it most certainly is a crime."

"Our vicar, that's Mr. Ellington, must've found the empty spots by acc'dent. Was right worried when he told folks at service two weeks ago. And then—" Rose leaned in to hear her new friend.

"But that' not the worst of it. Old feller, Mr. Denison, walked out one day to find his old spaniel's grave marker had been snitched. From 'is very yard. Nervy? Thugs, I call 'em. Prob'ly them technical kids. Thinking up all sorts of mischief."

"You've mentioned the 'technical kids' twice, Mary. Where is this technical school located? You've made me *very* curious about it."

"Them that's in the tech school, oh, maybe twenty kilometers from East Plumley. Prob'ly thought it was quite the prank to pull off."

"I would think that maybe they'd choose Swaffham for pranks or rabble-rousing. Isn't Swaffham a much larger town than East Plumley? More opportunities for fun?"

"Mebbe you're on to somthin', Miss. If not the techies, who, then? But law, look at the time; I best get back to bakin'."

"I've taken too much of your time, Mary, but I've loved our visit. If you have one more minute, would you happen to know where Mr. Denison lives? I need to pay him a visit."

"Do I indeed? I know every soul in East Plumley. Let me find a scrap of paper."

∽⊙⊚⊙∾

Rose returned to the High by eight o'clock. The dark clouds of the morning had lifted and although the day held little promise to be fair, a few scattered cumulous clouds parted to present patches of blue sky. Shopkeepers were opening doors and raising shutters. Greetings were exchanged across the broad street. Rose missed little and she enjoyed the obvious camaraderie of the town's tradesmen and women.

"Have a watch there, Madam." A string bean of a fellow wielding a long broom stopped Rose as she passed The Rose and Thistle.

He tipped his cap and bowed slightly. "Recognized you from the other evenin'. Deebs is the name. You was with the vicar and all."

"Mr. Deebs! So it is. I'm so glad to see you again. Our introduction to the pub was delightful. And delicious; you and the vicar were right about those shepherd's pies."

"Deebs it is. NO 'mister'. Pleased to have served you, Ma'am. Now, watch your step here; look lively at the water. Clean-up time at The Rose."

"Deebs, can you spare a moment? I'm terrible at names and we met so many lovely people last evening . . . that Mr. Penn-something. Does he live here in East Plumley?"

A solemn expression crossed Deebs' face. He muttered "Hope he weren't one of the lovely ones," changed expression and said "E'd be the town solicitor, Ma'am. Mr. Pennington checks taxes in and out, collects fines, manages to do smart bit of private business on the side. *Everyone* knows Mr. Pennington."

"A good man, I take it?"

Deebs paused before answering. "I think the vicar looks to Mr. P. for advice."

"Well, that is as good a reference as any, I would suppose. One more question, Deebs, if you can spare me a second—"

"Surely, Ma'am. You put me in mind of my old gran: 'Just one more thing, Deebs'?"

Rose laughed and replied, "Well, I *am* someone's 'old gran' back in the States, to twelve as a matter of fact. But my question, Deebs, is this: What sort of school is the technical college I've heard about? Do you know any of the young people who attend?"

"No Ma'am. They stay busy connected to them machines an' computers up there. East Plumley is too slow for those eggheads. Too slow and too small. Most of 'em live in Ely or Swaffham. We're slim pickins' for that lot."

"Thank you, Deebs. Oh, and one more person I must ask you about. The young man who caused the ruckus last evening. A Mr. Botts, I believe?"

"A bad 'un, Ma'am. Nothing but trouble for old Willem. Thought working at St. Michael's would help, but 'spect the vicar is having second thoughts about that now."

"You have been so helpful, Deebs. This has given me a bit more perspective on the town."

"Off now to have a look roun', are you?"

"Indeed. I really enjoy your English mornings. The air is so fresh…."

"Visitin' long, then?"

"Just passing through. Conducting a bit of church survey business. I hope I haven't taken too much of your time this morning, Deebs. I always have a bushel of questions and I've kept you from your chores. Not to worry, I'm out of your way now. Thank you."

Is it possible that Deebs knows something about those thefts? I didn't get the impression from talking to him that he is exactly brimming with curiosity. But he does see everything that goes on…

Gracious, look at that. I have found the village post office. It must be a part of this antique shop. Yes, the little flag tucked by the door says just that. The posies in the window match the yellow flag. I'll stop in for some stamps before I leave. Perhaps tomorrow. But I cannot resist a hardware shop. I'll just pop across the street for a quick look.

"Mornin', Missus. Yer up bright as sunshine this fine day. Welcome to Gresham and Gibbs, Tools and Others. What could I find for you this mornin'?"

"I'm not going to waste any of your time, Mr., um, Gibbs?"

"No mum: I'm Gresham. Gibbs passed thirty years ago. On me own now, aren't I?"

"That's two of us, Mr. Gresham: on our own. I'm glad to meet you. I'm Mrs. Rose McNess, from Virginia, in the States. And I won't waste any of your day. I enjoy poking around in hardware shops. The smell of all the new tools just, well, it's a smell like no other. And what a sweet cat. I believe it's smiling at me."

"So she is. That's Marigold. She doesn't take to all customers. You are a rare one, Madam. Take your time. Look around. Might just find something you need among all me shelves. Anything but Marigold." Wrapping the yellow tabby in his arms, Mr. Gresham chuckled heartily and walked slowly down the gardening aisle.

Rose, trailing behind, exclaimed, "Look at these new hoes, and a different kind of rake. I've never seen one with curved prongs. Where are these used, Mr. Gresham?"

"Under hedgerows. See how they curl? Got to reach 'ways back and pull all the winter out. Only twelve pounds for that one. Real bargain, 'tis."

"My partner would love to see that. She's just back from Australia and I'm sure they don't have a tool like that 'down under'. And what in the world is this sinister tool Mr. Gresham? It looks positively medieval."

"Sure, Mam, so it does. *French* medieval. This be a gimlet. Folks here in the village don't have fancy 'lectrics in their gardens, so gimlets the answer. They be drills, good for getting to the heart of dead wood, stubborn stumps, the like. Or just drilling a hole. Nothin's better than a gimlet in your tool pouch. And I carry three sizes. One you seized upon is the largest of the set."

"Gracious, these are awesome. I would take one home for my son if I thought I could get it through security. Alas, I know better than to even think about that."

"Tourists, are *ye?*"

"Actually, no. We're here as part of a church survey team, looking at different parishes in this part of East Anglia."

"Cannot fool old Gresham. Mind says you're here to look into headstones missin' from St. Michael's. Nasty business."

"Mr. Gresham, I cannot fib. The investigation is *part* of our survey. What's your idea about these thefts? I, rather, my partner and I need all the help we can get."

"Strangest bit to ever happen 'ere. We're a quiet village. Go about our business, raise our young 'uns, services on the Sabbath, pop over to The Rose for a pint. Nothing ruffles East Plumley. Bit of mischief has ever' one worried. Caused business here to fall off ever so slight."

"I'm sorry for that. You have one of the cleanest, most well-stocked hardware stores I've ever visited. How I wish my late husband could see this. He was absolutely nuts about tools and bolts and any sort of a mower. And this building is so impressive. Was it a large private home before it became a place of business?"

Am I talking too fast? Talking just to talk? I mustn't act as if I'm so involved in those thefts.

"Way before, Madam. Look outside the archway: house was divided into two parts 'round eighteen sixties. Grime & Garden's there now. It's a good fit: folks buy pots and plants, come over to Gresham for tools and soil. Yes'm, a good fit."

"Mr. Gresham, you have made my morning a real delight. I've so enjoyed chatting with you, and Marigold. I hope the rest of your day is wonderful. Goodbye!"

Mr. Gresham grinned, put Marigold down on a stack of burlap bags and waved briskly as his visitor from the States smiled and continued with her walk.

This is so pleasant, mused Rose. Different country, different traditions. But people are people the world over, no matter where one goes. Pride in one's hometown, fearful of threats to their security. Everyone has basically the same goals: a job they enjoy, a decent living, family happiness. Makes me wonder how life is back at Wynfield Farms today. Why, I could easily have been chatting with Ed at the Fincastle Hardware in Virginia, choosing bulbs to plant around the Wynfield entrance. Mr. Gresham was so friendly and patient, explaining those unique tools he sells. And he's obviously proud of East Plumley, always a sign of a good citizen. Well, I'd better stop woolgathering and get on to Mr. Denison's.

Mary's directions brought a smile to Rose's face and her feet to #27 Chewning Street.

"Mr. Denison?" The door opened at first knock. "I'm Rose McNess and I've heard of your recent trouble. The *theft*. I… I'm on church business but may I come in and chat a moment?"

Forgive me, Lord! I had to say something legitimate so the poor man would let me in the house. Isn't it sort of church business? Therlowe Denison smiled tentatively at the slight woman in a pale green twin set and tweeds standing before him. His wild, bushy eyebrows rose above clear blue eyes. The longer he stared at his visitor the wider the smile spread across his face.

"Come in, come in!" Mr. Denison bowed slightly and ushered Rose into his small sitting room.

"I promise not to take all your morning, Mr. Denison. I would like to hear about your theft. Do you recall when it happened?"

Therlowe Denison hunched into his worn recliner, settling himself to think about his robbery. Rose's eyes darted from corner to corner in the overstuffed room.

Obviously, a widower. Can't bring himself to part with anything. Pillows, knick- knacks, a spoon collection. How many spoons could one person collect in a lifetime? Wonderful old piano. Bet the wife played that instrument - will be a monster to move if he decides to sell it. Place is clean as a pin; probably has a 'daily' who comes in to—

"February 21. This past month. Early morning. I came in from The Rose the night of the 20th. Bit of a celebration 'til the pub closed. Sonny was perfectly sound at that time. Yes, February 21. This year." .

"And you've had no visitor, no tradesmen before that date?"

"Oh, no. This house, my front garden, been here sixty years. Sonny's been in the back there for about thirteen. Mind you, I've been here sixty. Know every soul walks by, walks in. Property's intact. I've got m'deed if you care to see it."

"Oh, no, that won't be necessary, Mr. Denison. Just checking the facts and they are exactly what the vicar had relayed. In your memory, has anyone suspicious been hanging around? And can you think of any reason why someone would *want* your pet's grave marker?" Therlowe Denison scratched his rather large red nose and shook his head vigorously.

"Never. Never in m'life have I seen anything so foolish. That's what I told vicar. I guess that's how you've come to call. Investigate, that is. Word around that two American ladies here to help Coulton. Is that what you're about, Mrs.?"

"McNess. Mrs. Rose McNess. I wasn't completely honest with you when I barged in, was I? But there are two of us visiting to attend to some other church business at St. Michael's. And since you *are* a member of the parish, your theft certainly concerns us. And as I am a dog lover, well, I couldn't help but be intrigued by your loss. I've buried five Scotties, Mr. Dennison. It gives me such a pain in my heart to think that their resting places would be disturbed. It's so…so unnecessary. And so evil."

Golly. I hope I sound convincing. How did word get around so quickly that two American ladies are here to help? It is always thus: word does spread in village, large or small.

"Nothing will bring Sonny back. He was the best. Fourteen years. But it would settle my heart to have that little piece of memory returned. Now, if you will excuse me, I must tend to my bees. Good day, Mrs. McNabb." With that, Therlowe Denison rose, extended his hand to Rose McNess and showed her to the door.

And a good day to you Mr. Denison—Mrs. McNabb will be on her way! Now there's a man who knows how to live: a pint or two at the pub of a night, a leisurely day in his favorite chair, and to cap the day's business, a session with his bees. Golly, I will bet that East Plumley has more than a few Therlowe Denisons living here—and living well.

If I had a bicycle I would spend the rest of my day discovering every corner of this village. But—I don't, so off I go to learn the 'mystery of the missing gate stop'.

✑✑✑

Chapter Sixteen

Rose reached in her pocket for the scrap of paper she needed. 16 Willow Lane. Should've asked Mary how to find Willow. Well, it can't be far. There's not that much territory in East Plumley. It might even be one of the streets off the Green.

Rose's walk from Mr. Denison's had taken her to the Village Green at the south end of the High. The Green was a neat, grassy square, pristine save for the worn footpath that severed it diagonally from north to south. Surrounding the Green on three sides were predictably tidy, terraced asymmetrical houses in a similar architectural style that Rose could only describe as 'late Georgian'.

St. Michael's in the Cedars appeared sheltered, even hidden, off the fourth side.

I'm tempted to stop . . . do I dare? I'm right here. I'm sure Amaryllis and Vicar are working in his office or among the gravestones. I don't want to look as if I am snooping. Oh, why not? I'll just pop inside for a moment to have a look-see at this lovely old church.

Rose strode to the porch and saw that one of the heavy doors was ajar. She pushed lightly and entered the cool, dim interior that was redolent with the scents of cedar and musky incense.

Exactly what I had envisioned: center aisle, boxed pews, hand-carved arm rests. Probably one pew per family from the original congregants. And it does have a stained-glass window, right above the altar. What a lovely Madonna and Babe .... must be glorious when the morning sun shines through. If the bonnet doesn't block all the light. What a creation! Now THAT is a bonnet. I'm rather surprised there isn't anything written about it in some of the regional literature I've read. Guess Ely Cathedral is the prize in these parts. I'm going to have to find out more about the bonnet's history. Whoops!

"Sorry, young man, I was talking to myself .... "

Rose looked down at a crumpled figure in wrinkled khaki who suddenly popped up from the pew in front of her.

"Not s'possed to be in here. Church's closed."

"I'm just leaving, young man. I would ask *you* to consider who's trespassing! "

Rose turned and marched indignantly from St. Michael's.

That must be 'Trouble', Botts' nephew. If he is being paid to sleep on the job I would say the vicar—and Botts—need to keep an eye on him.

Golly, would you look at the time? Must move along to the gate stop but sure am glad I had a peek at St. Michael's. A bit disturbing about that young man, but right now I best concentrate on where I am supposed to be going. I'll just keep looking at street signs.

A short walk along Willow brought Rose to a neatly lettered, if weathered, sign bearing the numeral 16. She looked over a low stonewall that defined the humble yard to see a woman brandishing a pair of large and lethal secateurs. The woman was short and wiry with gray hair that rose from her scalp as if it had been electrified.

Rose decided that as an innocent passerby she was in no danger. Nevertheless, she moved cautiously through the small gate that was hanging forlorn and limp.

"Madam! Madam, may I have a word?"

The woman stopped her attack and glared at Rose.

"Don't call me a madam! Who are you? What do you want? You can see I'm in the middle of a project."

"I hate to interrupt but I am here to help. Help with the loss of your gate stop. If you could spare five minutes—"

"Oh, hell! I don't give a fig about the bloody gate stop! And WHO are you?"

"I'm Rose McNess from Virginia, and I am—"

"You 're one of those church ladies I've heard about. Oh, come on in. I can spare five minutes. No more. Come, come! Sit here on the step and I'll continue with my tree."

Delighted at the shift in the wind, Rose smiled her most benign smile. Walking vigorously, she crossed the lawn and sat on the doorstep as the woman indicated.

"Sorry I yelled. Determined to get it down today."

"Is it diseased?" ventured Rose.

"Hell, no! It's just the wrong sort. Never should've planted it here. But you didn't come from the States to discuss my tree. I'm Mimslyn Welford. Your name, again? And why *did* you come?"

"I'm Rose. Rose McNess, and you are correct. I *am* 'one of the church ladies' from the States. I, rather, *we,* as there are two of us, are here on a church survey, and through that are involved with St. Michael's. The vicar has told us about the thefts in town and that has piqued my interest. In a nutshell, that is why I am here. To hear about *your* loss. And please, do call me 'Rose'."

"Hardly a thing of value. Its usefulness was holding the damn gate closed."

"Was it very old?"

"Of course it was old! My place is old, with an old wall and an older gate. I'm old! But why someone would take that particular 'old' defies me! Covered with grime and lichen—"

Rose interrupted: "Lichen?"

"Did you notice the gate when you came through? Yard is much lower there. Water collects after rains. Lichen collected on the gate stop. Can't see lichen making the damn stop more valuable to a thief."

"Have you noticed any unusual people walking by or hanging about, night or day?"

"No, and I wouldn't, would I? I'm usually back here, inside or outside"

Rose mulled over before asking, "Do you think this, well, *stealing,* is something relatively rare in East Plumley?"

"Quite. Most folks living here are decent, hard-working, been here for years. I don't care for many folks, including my neighbors, but that doesn't mean they're not good people. I don't have to like 'em to live among them, do I? And thievery? No, not much of that in the town. More 'n likely the young ones from the technical college."

Rose paused. This was the third time she'd heard 'technical college' mentioned.

"Will you replace the stop?"

"Oh, yes. Young Botts comes 'round now and then, looking to earn a pound or so. Haven't seen much of him since he started helping at St. Michael's. When he's of a mind, he'll show up. Speed isn't a large part of life in East Plumley, which you may have discovered. Staying at The Arms, are you?"

"Oh, yes. It is delightful. And we fell in love with your town as we drove in from London."

"Let old Giles fill you in on most of the town's doins'. He's been here for an eternity. If there's stealing or hijinks in East Plumley, Giles will know."

"Speaking of which, I've been here for an eternity. You've been very kind and I apologize for taking up so much of your time."

"Needed a rest, didn't I?"

"And so did your poor tree!" Rose said to herself.

Rose waved again as Mimslyn Welford returned to the devastation of her tree. That tree is in for it now. Gracious, look at the hour: nearly half-past twelve. I hope I didn't wear out my welcome. Time got away from me, let's see, she said the stream was at the end of Willow. I'll meander on down to see if I can piece together anything about the missing millstone.

Because East Plumley encompassed one of the flattest areas of already-flat East Anglia, most of the residential areas were similar in plan. If the landscape varied by a meter or two here and there, builders compensated by varying the architecture of the homes they constructed. This was particularly noticeable on Willow Lane.

Rose McNess strolled along this quiet neighborhood on a worn and wide tree- lined footpath that bordered both sides of the street. She paused to look at the diminutive front yards in front of houses that ranged in style of 18th century Georgian to one or two that shouted Neo-classical and even pseudo-Gothic. Several semi-detached homes and smaller bungalows nestled comfortably alongside their neighbors. No matter the architecture, each yard boasted an apron of a garden or a swath of lawn or both, that was, even in mid-March, healthy and green. Rose noted that the bordering trees, when in leaf, would provide umbrellas of shade. These same trees, bare now, still provided cover if someone, or *ones,* were on a mission to steal a gate stop or a millstone.

Because she was so thoroughly enchanted with the neighborhood and was imagining the occupant of every house, Rose reached what Mrs. Welford had dubbed, "Plum's Stream" in less than half an hour.

There were two benches on the bank overlooking the stream. A freshly turned earthen area separated the benches.

Aha! That's the site. The millstone rested between the benches. Why on earth a millstone when there's no mill and the stream is merely a trickle? Guess that's why it was concrete-ornamental. Great view. I can even see a church spire in the distance. Possibly Swaffham? Have to look into that … but this millstone! I won't get any clues if I just stand and look at it, will I? Bet folks used this stone as a side table. They'd sit on the benches, place their canteens on the stone and gaze at the view. Well, only thing I can do today is measure the imprint. Must say the thief did a neat removal job, all very precise. No jagged edges.

Rose removed a tape from her purse and kneeled to measure the diameter. When she pressed the tape to ground her right index finger hit a sliver of something hard.

"Ouch! What is this? Damn thing cut my finger." Rose looked at her bloody digit.

"Piece of metal. Bent, perhaps from a clasp of some kind. This could have been here for years *or* our thief may have lost it. Some jackets close with clasps. And so do backpacks. Golly. Progress, even a little. Makes me want to get to the heart of this mystery. Am I talking to myself? Yes, Rose, you are. Time to get back to Amaryllis and reality. She has to have made progress this morning."

Chapter Seventeen

"Whew, Giles, I am, as we say in Virginia, 'tuckered out.'"

"Enjoying your walkabout in East Plumley, Madam?"

"Very much Giles. But let me ask you something. I stopped to chat with a Mimslyn Welford. Do you happen to know her? She's a delightful character."

Giles reddened, *harrumphed,* and offered: "There's some in East Plumley who would have other words for Mrs. Welford. Did she offer to show you her vast collection of rare Spode teapots?"

"No," replied Rose.

"Pity," Giles harrumphed again.

"Oh, I rather think her bark is worse than her bite. And I did catch her at a busy time. But she mentioned a technical school nearby. I'm curious, Giles, do you know much about that, or how close it is to East Plumley?"

"That would be, Madam, the 'Swaffham-Lynn Technical College'. Very superior institute for engineers. Located a bit north of Swaffham, closer to King's Lynn. It has been said-*harrumph*-requirements for the College are much more difficult than those required for Cambridge."

"Oh, my! I don't suppose many of *those* students would find East Plumley very exciting, would you?"

"Hardly, Madam. Swaffham, King's Lynn, Norwich are far more exciting destinations for the young."

"That just leaves more of East Plumley for visitors such as Dr. Keynes-Livingston and me to enjoy, doesn't it? Well, I better stop wasting your time and get on up to our suite. Thank you, Giles, for the information."

Surely that eliminates students from the technical school raising any kind of a ruckus in East Plumley. I could investigate further but I think old Giles would have let something slip if he had a clue about these recent thefts.

∽ઓᏮᏉᏅ

Rose picked up her key from the desk and turned to go upstairs. As she turned toward the lift she noticed Kevin hunched in a corner toward the Dining Salon, his normally immaculate uniform, filthy. Though the lad was lost in the intricacies of the cell phone in his hand Rose could see that his face was red and swollen.

Rose had hoped to have a chat with Kevin but this was not the opportune moment. She decided a bit of mothering might be in order.

"Kevin! I hoped I would run into you. But . . . my dear, *what* in the world has happened to you? Let me have a look at that eye!"

"Oh, its nothin', Ms., really, nothin'. Just let me be, please."

"Absolutely not, Kevin. Here, step into the Salon. No one's about and I can see that eye in a proper light. And Giles is busy at the desk if you're worried about *that.*"

"Oooo, Giles will have me head if he sees me this way. I'll go get m'other suit and wash m'face. Eye's gone down a bit, hasn't it, Miss?"

"It is a bit swollen, but not black and blue. Cold water will do the trick I'm thinking. Try to keep a cold tissue on it for a bit. Can you tell me what happened, or would you rather not talk about it, Kevin?"

Rose had her hands on the teenager's shoulders and was looking into his red and frightened eyes.

He's really a scared little boy! More afraid of Giles...or of me?

"'T'was Trouble."

"What trouble, Kevin?"

"No Mum; *Trouble* Botts. Tried to get me to snatch a pack of cigs for 'im from BIBBS'. When I said 'No!', he let me 'ave it."

"You mean 'BIBBS', the grocers?"

"One and the same. I come to work that way and Trouble was waitin' there at the corner. Just waitin' for some sucker like me to come 'long."

"Well, congratulations, Kevin. You were NOT the sucker of the day! I'm proud to know that you stood up to him. I've only been in East Plumley a short while, but even I have heard of Trouble Botts. Do you think he just hangs around looking for ways to cause mischief?"

"Oh, no, Miss. Trouble's got somethin' going for 'im. Some days 'e's got the chips; others, liken today, not a penny."

Although Rose was anxious for Kevin to tend to his eye, she was also intrigued by his take on the elusive Trouble.

"Do you think he is a member of a gang? Is that a crazy question, Kevin? Are there even gangs in East Plumley?"

"Hardly gangs, Miss. No gang would touch Trouble even if there were any. 'E's just a bad one, Miss. Now—"

"Sorry, Kevin, go tend to that eye. It looks better already. And do change your uniform; you look splendid when you're all dressed to receive guests. And don't worry, I'll not breathe a word to old Giles."

As tempted as she was to embrace the teenager in a fierce hug, Rose merely patted Kevin's shoulder and watched him walk toward the loo.

Rose reflected on her interview. What a sweetheart! Teenagers steal my heart: he so reminds me of my grandsons. But that Trouble! He certainly has earned the name. I'll just tuck this little incident away for future reference.

An exuberant Amaryllis greeted Rose at the door of their suite.

"Rose, darling—am I glad to see you! Come in, come in! I'm just finishing my tea. Join me and we can catch up on our morning's work. Let me tell you, it is damp and *cold* in St. Michael's churchyard. Very March like. Brrrr! But we—"

"Slow down, Amaryllis, slow down, you've been up and running a lot longer than I. Let's just sit here and relax. I've got a bit of news, but it can wait. We've got all afternoon to share finds. First, I would like a bit of tea, if there is any more to be had."

"Of course! It's quite hot, and jasmine. Your favorite. Sandwich to go with?"

"Let me sit and sip first."

"Well, while you are sitting and sipping I shall fill you in on our vicar. The Reverend Coulton Ellington is from Winchester, England, a public-school man, educated at Cambridge. Widower with two children, both married, living in Australia, has been in East Plumley for sixteen years, has two children—"

"Stop! You've already enumerated his children. Amaryllis, did you badger the poor man? I bet he said 'Australia' and that set you off. Was all this conversation between the gravestones?"

"Absolutely not. It was so cold when I arrived at the church that the vicar invited me in for coffee by the fire. I accepted and we must have talked for an hour. I think he's lonely, Rose, Or rather, lonely for conversation with a *real* woman."

Rose hooted, "A *real* woman! That you ARE, Amaryllis!" Rose chuckled and wiped away tears of laughter. She grinned at her irrepressible friend.

"Don't deny it, Rose, you know exactly what I mean. I *am* a woman of the world, talk knowledgeably about Australia, (where his children are!), and I am certainly not going to woo him with a gummy casserole, or coax him into bed."

"I certainly hope not. And leave me to find our thief? Say it isn't so, Amaryllis!" They both laughed and put down their cups simultaneously.

"Fun's over, Amaryllis. Tell me what else you learned this morning. Out of the office and in the churchyard."

"First things first: the entire area behind St. Michael's is a lichen repository. And mostly the same species. It is virtually a greenhouse: humid, still air, patches of sun filtering through leaves, soil that retains the damp. I collected over twelve slides of lichen and popped them into the minibar, in perfect condition." Amaryllis indicated the worn navy bag crumpled beside the small fridge.

Rose asked, "How can you be sure this is the same kind of lichen that was on the stolen gravestones?"

"Well, I have no way of knowing precisely, but given the same environment and the same host, I would say that I can be 99% sure of my findings. But that's not all."

"There's more?"

"Mr. Blakely finally appeared!"

"Ah, the elusive curate. Tell all: what was *he* like?"

"Rather shy young man. He's not unattractive, really. About the vicar's height, on the thin side, shock of reddish hair. Has a narrow face, a bit melancholy, sad. But his carriage. Oh, I longed to say to him, 'Hold your shoulders up!'"

"I am surprised you didn't!"

"I'm not that uncivil, Rose. It was hard enough getting any answers out of him as it was. If I had criticized his posture he probably would have fled. I had him walk me through the churchyard and point out where the headstones had been. He did that, silently, and once we reached the last spot, he turned and left. Just left."

"I call that rude."

"I am trying to be charitable to the fellow, but I agree. Other than giving his name, where he studied, and the fact that he'd only been at St. Michael's for eight months, that is *all* the information I got out of him."

"Did you ask Reverend Ellington about him? Or did you have a chance?"

"We talked about Stewart Blakely while we were having our coffee. And yes, I instigated the talk. Apparently, the young man had spent two years in New Guinea and returned to Great Britain to attend to family matters. Death of a grandparent or something. After that he started applying for pastoral positions and ended up here in East Plumley. Seems the former Curate had just been ordained and called to another parish. I got the distinct impression that the vicar is still, after eight months, feeling a bit uneasy about the choice."

"Does he not trust the fellow?"

"Oh, he says he is fine with the offices of the church, pleasant enough with members, preaches a fair sermon when called upon. He trusts him but he cannot deny he has a feeling about him. Particularly when Blakely goes off during the day with no explanation."

"That's not a good thing, particularly in a small parish."

"The vicar realizes that he must do something about this. He's received no complaints from parishioners; it's his 'gut feeling' that bothers him. And I have to admit, after my walk with him in the cold, I share that feeling. But enough of my morning. Your turn. Tell me everything you've discovered in East Plumley, Rose."

"I've just had a most informative conversation with Giles. I'll tell you about that later. But I've done nothing as exciting as chatting with the vicar. I did meet four of East Plumley's real characters. Two filled me in on their respective thefts. No clue from either, no lichen to present. But I do have what might be a piece of evidence, or a *clue,* from the thief. Of course, I may die of blood poisoning but it will be for a good cause—"

"Your finger! What did you do, Rose?"

Rose reached in her pocket and fished out the scrap of tissue with the small metal clasp.

"Here is my clue! Either prehistoric Iron Age or half a clasp from a jacket or backpack. What do you think?"

Amaryllis held the metal clasp up to the strongest light in the room and said, "Sorry, old dear, it is *not* prehistoric anything. It's *our* age and probably from a shop in the local mall. And good eyes, Rose. It is definitely half a clasp from what I would guess is a jeans jacket. You know the kind: all the young ones wear them. It narrows our field of suspects. All we have to do now is look closely at the coats we encounter."

"This is barely a start. We still don't have any idea why someone is stealing these things."

"We've been here barely forty-eight hours, Rose. My brain is working overtime and so is yours. May I suggest that we take a break from our problem solving and rest our gray cells. Then we will be up for another night at the pub. And *do* put a plaster on that finger."

౿෨෧෨ఽ

Chapter Eighteen

Refreshed from their nap the two sleuths decided it was time to experience dining out in East Plumley. Back to back evenings at the pub might present more questions than they were prepared to answer

"Vicar told me that **BIRYANI** is quite nice. Authentic curry."

"Did he really?" asked Rose, suppressing a smile.

Amaryllis, busily twisting her hair into its customary chignon, never heard the sarcasm.

"How about it, Rose, fancy a curry?"

"Sounds like a plan, dear. It'll be fun to explore the culinary resources of East Plumley."

When the pair arrived in the lobby, Giles beamed from his post behind the desk.

"Good evening, ladies. I trust everything is to your satisfaction?"

"Giles, everything is perfect. We could not be more content."

"And your survey, your church work, is it progressing as you hope?"

"Indeed. And now we are treating ourselves to a night on the town. Can you recommend the spot for curry for two hungry Americans?"

"I rarely indulge in non-native nourishment, ladies. We have one foreign establishment in East Plumley. I've heard from, shall I say, *younger* visitors, that **BIRYANI** is quite good. Dangerously hot condiments but acceptable in every other respect."

"Well," chuckled Rose, "We may just go and try **BIRYANI** and forego the spicy bits. To find this spot, do we turn left or right on the High, Giles?"

"Take a left from the front entrance, Mesdames. Your keys, please?" Rose and Amaryllis deposited their keys, waved and walked out as directed.

⋘◉⋙

Giles Bertram Hurlbert turned to the front window and watched as the two American ladies made their way down the High in search of Indian cuisine.

Returning to the desk he shook his head slowly and thought about his visitors' quest. Could I honestly recommend an Indian restaurant? Could I recommend any non-native establishment? Certainly not! Simple, plain, wholesome

English fare is more than adequate. Our Dining Salon right here in The Arms has what—a three-star rating? Should be five, certainly on the nights when Chef brings out the sea food specialties . . . and the filets. Indeed, gourmet, without traipsing off to a foreigner's kitchen.

I do say I was fair in reference to BIRYANI's. That younger set, two weeks ago, was it? Weren't they the ones that returned all smiles about the curries they encountered. No doubt Mesdames McNess and Keynes-Livingston will be satisfied.

Two different sorts, those ladies. Of course, provenance is all. Missus McNess is from Virginia. Everyone I've encountered from that state has been civil. Quite civil. And the other one, Doctor Keynes-Livingston: just returned from Australia? Consorting with who-knows-what sorts out there. She's a curious one. Returning each day with that canvas carry-all of hers jiggling and bulging with oddities. Who knows what these ladies are up to.

Giles yawned, stretched his long arms over his head, and yawned again. He patted the remaining hairs on his balding pate, straightened his tie, checked that the buttons on his blazer were properly aligned, and lowered himself onto the hard-back and high chair that was his alone: his throne at The Plumley Arms.

This was the time of the evening that Giles savored. Most of the guests were dining in the Salon. He felt confident that the two visiting "church ladies" would be home within two hours. No guests were expected to arrive this evening if advance reservations were to be believed. Ah, Ely will be hopping tonight. Their hostelry undoubtedly will be full. Cathedral concert. Pity East Plumley cannot compete. But then, I do prefer the quiet pulse of our village. We march to a steady rhythm of steadfast English values. Indeed.

Giles pulled out a worn and creased paperback of crossword puzzles. There were few unfilled pages, but he shuffled through until he found one.

But I really do not want crosswords tonight. Why have I got the service on my mind? Guess it was the obit in today's *Times*. Old Dennis, gone at 94. Man was best in my company; we medaled together, din't we? Den had no family. Guess he was better off there at the Chelsea' vets home. Always liked being near the Thames. Think we talked about bunking together when it was all over. How could we even think it would be over with the shells falling all around us for weeks? Hell. Hell it was. That part of Germany was pure hell. Den got it in the leg. Wonder he din't lose it. Lucky. Me? I was the lucky one. Retreated here, back home. The "Plum's" no 'Thames' but it suits me!

Wouldn't those American ladies be surprised if 'Old Giles' pulled out a medal for them to see? No fooling Old Giles. Both those ladies think I've had no life other than standing behind this desk to hand out keys and advice about foreign eateries. Little do they know; little do they know!

Lost in reveries of his past and thoughts of his wartime buddy, Giles allowed his shoulders to slump and his eyes to close. But just for a moment: it was his lot to be the keeper of the castle.

⋘◉⋙

"I would love to stuff him with some 'dangerously hot condiments', wouldn't you, Rose?"

Rose laughed and replied, "Amaryllis, you are terrible! Nothing would shake old Giles. He's a warrior straight from the pages of Gibbons' **Decline and Fall of the Roman Empire.**"

"Why Rose, I am impressed! All this time I thought your literary interests were much more ephemeral."

"Amaryllis, I don't read textbooks, but I *do* read more than 'romance novels'. And I *do* keep up with world affairs through a variety of media. I am not mentally suffocating at Wynfield Farms as you seem to imply."

"I'm sorry Rose. You know what a prig I can be sometimes. Please forgive me."

They laughed, and walked left down High Street in the evening light. All the shops were beginning to close even as people bustled in and out to finish last minute errands or buy one more item for tea. A short line waited at the butcher shop and Mary's Own looked crowded.

BIRYANI was not hard to spot: fairy lights twinkled over the arched doorway and canned music could be heard long before the two reached the entrance. A jovial gentleman in Punjabi garb greeted Rose and Amaryllis as they hesitated at the door.

"Welcome, beautiful ladies! Welcome to my humble eatery. I promise you, the best Indian food in all British Isles. Come in, come in!"

The portly fellow's melodic voice and the tantalizing aromas wafting on the air hurried the women through the doorway.

A younger man appeared from the dim interior and asked, "Two for supper? This way, please, to serve you well. Please watch step—"

Amaryllis whispered to Rose, "I've never smelled anything as heavenly in my life. It's almost intoxicating! What do you suppose they are cooking?"

"We'll soon find out: here comes our fellow with menus. And hot towels."

"Please, to cleanse one's hands," he directed, placing the steaming linens in front of each woman. "And to cleanse the palate? A beverage? May I suggest?"

"We'll have tea, please. Could you bring a large pot for the two of us? And do tell us your name, young man. I do like to know with whom I am speaking." Amaryllis spoke softly and precisely as she directed her questions to the handsome young man, who now looked as if he would bring the entire kitchen to Amaryllis if she but crooked a finger.

"I am Seva, and I shall have the distinct honor of being your server for the evening."

"Thank you, Seva. And when you return with our *very* large, *very* hot pot of tea, we shall have looked over the menu and will be prepared to put our trust-and our appetites-in your hands!" With this approbation Seva beamed, white teeth gleaming in his dark and glistening face, then bowed out of the room to disappear behind the enveloping curtain at the rear of the restaurant.

"I must say you made quite an impression on that young man, Amaryllis. He'll be yours for life . . . or at least the duration of our meal tonight."

"He has a sweet face. I trust him. Isn't it remarkable how one can just *tell* about people?"

"Some of the time, dear, some of the time. Now, what do you recommend? There's a little bit of everything here."

"Well, from looking over the menu I can see that the proprietors are from the Punjab, the northern part of India. My favorite. Let's start with Mulligatawny soup, and naan, that marvelous bread. Then I'm going with the Lamb Rogan Josh. It's in a Kashmiri sauce, with a clove flavor. What about you, Rose?"

"Soup sounds perfect. Let's see. I believe I'll try the chicken curry, with mango and ginger sauce. Doesn't *that* sound divine? And look, at the bottom of the menu: 'Tell your waiter you wish it mild, medium, hot, or Indian hot'. We'll have to pass this little nugget on to old Giles."

A smiling Seva and a large, steaming pot of jasmine tea arrived minutes later; menus were read and dispensed, and before the pair had time to wonder where their day had gone, steaming platters were set before them. Seva, still smiling, popped lids off token dishes of spicy accompaniments, brought fresh naan, and bowed himself out once again.

"We'll never want to go home, Rose! My lamb is divine. English lamb in Indian garb. I'm heartless and hungry."

"And my curry is perfect. Mild, just as I asked. How can we be enjoying ourselves this innocently when we're here to uncover something so bad?"

"Bad, *and* devious. I've got to do more peering at those slides. Tonight if that lamp in our room is bright enough. This particular lichen I've found evidences some element, some chemical, some iteration that baffles me. It must be the fungus' relationship with the local concrete used in all the stolen items. Thank you for coming with me tonight, Rose. If we'd gone to the pub, as I know you would prefer, we could never just sit and talk and—"

Amaryllis stopped in mid-sentence and focused on the trio of young men who were now entering **BIRYANI**.

Seva approached the trio and beckoned them to follow him to a table close to the rear of the small restaurant.

"Amaryllis, you look positively stricken. Afraid we'll lose Seva to the newcomers?"

"Rose, Stewart Blakely. He's one of the three men that just walked in the door. We are staying for dessert."

Rose, momentarily stunned by her friend's remarks, glanced quickly toward the back of the restaurant where the trio was being seated.

"No, no, don't look at them, Rose. Let's remain *undiscovered* for the time being."

"They were busy getting seated, Amaryllis, and not looking our way. You certainly described Stewart Blakely to a 'T'. That red hair makes him stand out like a street light in the dark! Not to mention the contrast with his two companions."

"Isn't that just so," murmured Amaryllis.

"I think," began Rose, "that we have an ally in our *friend, your* friend, Seva. We could quietly question him about the other customers, not just those three. And then…."

"Perfect, let's start when he clears our plates. He's coming now"

"Seva, that was delicious. Is **BIRYANI** open every night of the week? I know we'll want to come again."

"Thank you, Madam. **BIRYANI** closes only on Monday. Do not come on Sundays, as that is our busiest day.

Families come from all over for buffet. Too many children for Seva."

They all laughed, then Rose asked quietly, "Is this one of your busiest nights, Seva? All the tables are occupied—"

"Just normal, Madam"

"Everyone seems to be very comfortable here; that's important. And young. Do most of your patrons come from East Plumley, or other towns around here?" Amaryllis sat beaming at her partner and Seva, biding her time before entering the conversation.

"I thought I recognized one of your customers, Seva: the tall fellow with red hair who just walked in. I *believe* he's new at the parish church. Would you happen to know?"

Once more Seva beamed his spotlight smile. "Madam is correct. Mr. Blakely. One of our regulars. Comes in for vegetarian and Indian hot. And one beer. Good fellow!"

"And his friends: are they regulars, also?"

"Oh no, Madam. Mr. Blakely always alone. Tonight first time. They not part of East Plumley. Seva has never seen Mr. Blakely's friends."

"I met Mr. Blakely this morning at St. Michael's. I might just pop over and say hello to him before we leave. We'll finish our tea but you can bring the check any time, Seva."

"You changed your mind about dessert?" asked Rose.

"Mr. Blakely will be our dessert: the perfect finish to a scrumptious meal."

Rose and Amaryllis neatly divided the check, and left Seva a handsome tip.

They gathered their wraps and walked casually to Stewart Blakely's table.

"Mr. Blakely. I knew I liked you: we've both a taste for Indian cuisine. Probably don't remember: Dr. Keynes-Livingston, from our brief visit this morning in the cold churchyard. My friend, Mrs. McNess." Rose nodded appropriately as the obviously uncomfortable Mr. Blakely struggled to rise.

"Oh, oh, yes. Dr. Keynes-Livingston. Nice to see you here. Indeed, Indian food. My favorite."

Blakely's two companions neither moved nor smiled. Obviously Stewart Blakely was on his own in handling the interruption.

"Do you and your friends come here often?" Rose asked innocently.

The two men remained seated. And silent.

Stewart Blakely saved his friends: "Well, we prefer **BIRYANI**, but we don't come here too often."

"I hope you have as lovely a meal as we just enjoyed, Mr. Blakely. Goodbye! I'm sure I'll see you at St. Michael's tomorrow." Amaryllis deftly got the parting shot into the conversation as she and Rose waved goodbye to Seva and left the restaurant.

The tinkling music followed them halfway up the High.

"Now, Rose, let's hear what you think about our elusive curate."

"Amaryllis. I'm too well fed and sleepy to be curious. In the morning, dear."

Chapter Nineteen

"Rose! Rose! Wake up!"

Rose raised her head and peered at the alarm: three o'clock.

"Rose! Rose! Please—" She was not dreaming: Amaryllis *was* calling her at three o'clock in the morning. Rose struggled to crawl out of the duvet's warm nest. She staggered to open her bedroom door.

"Amaryllis! What in the world?"

Amaryllis, aka Dr. Frances Keyes-Livingston, Doctor of Biology and Physical Sciences with specialty in Lichenology stood triumphantly at Rose's door. Amaryllis' peignoir enveloped her in a zodiac of neon: a kaleidoscopic rainbow.

Oh my Lord, the vestal virgin with the lamp, thought Rose. She suppressed the urge to giggle, knowing that Amaryllis was deathly serious.

"I've isolated it, Rose! Took most of the night but I did it! Hated to wake you up but I couldn't wait until morning. Thought I had lost my way."

"Amaryllis dear, I'm groggy, let me sit down. Of course you haven't lost your way. You have a makeshift lab with a borrowed scope and terrible lighting. I'm surprised you can see a slide, much less figure out what's on it. Please explain what it is that you've managed to isolate."

"Sorry. I know it's the middle of the night. I'll go slowly. I've tried several taxonomic methodologies and one particular lichen—one of the *acarospora*— grows here in East Anglia and is one of the ingredients in *ink*. Voila! I think we may call the guilty party, rather our most valued ingredient, rospora. But it's too common to make it worth stealing... must be something else."

"Rospora for Rose. A cheerful name for ink. Nice double-entendre, too!"

Amaryllis chuckled and continued. "Whoever is purging East Plumley of its artifacts knows this lichen and something about the structure of the sub-species that thrives on concrete. The lichen has to have some property the thieves want. Somehow, the thieves are extracting a minute substance from the algae. It is so fragile that they-the criminals-can't just scrape the lichen off the headstone or the gate stop and pack it away. The 'jewel' in the algae must be separated carefully and kept cold. *Very* cold."

"And that slide in your hand?"

"A bit of the algae that I have separated and put under the 'scope. I cannot tell the exact composites because I don't have all the proper chemicals, but it is radically different from what one expects. I am positive this is the key to the thefts. Could they be making ink from this combination? And why?"

"Golly! You were right from the beginning Amaryllis. We know that none of the missing pieces are worth more than a few pounds. It's what's *on* these pieces that's so valuable. You've found the *why* in the case and it's up to me to ferret out the *who*. No telling how much money these thugs are collecting. And the East Plumley thugs are just the little guys. They are supplying someone with a valuable substance that could—"

"I'm thinking the worst, Rose. If this harmless little alga has something a terrorist needs for a weapon of mass destruction or a poisonous gas . . . oh, God! This is too dreadful to contemplate."

"Or it could be a component in a cure for cancer? We can't contemplate: we have to stop this. And by that I mean stopping the thieves among us *now.*"

Rose shuddered and then glanced toward the door of the suite where a large envelope lay on the floor. "Amaryllis, look, we have a message. Giles must have placed it under our door after we went to bed last evening."

"While I was so totally engrossed with my slides I never noticed. Let's see what it is." Amaryllis opened the envelope and read aloud, "Dear Dr. Keynes-Livingston: Sorry to bother you at this late hour but could use your immediate assistance in the morning (Thurs, Mar 15). Many calls regarding thefts have come in since you left St. Michael's. OAP meeting 10:00AM and thought excellent opportunity to explain to those present WHAT is going on. Boost Morale and all that. Could you and your charming friend come and spend time with OAP's to calm waters?

"Coulton Ellington (Rev.)"

"Well, *'charming friend',* laughed Amaryllis, "I'll pack this slide away in the mini-fridge for now. Best we get back to bed to finish our beauty sleep in order to charm and calm those OAP's in the morning!"

Chapter Twenty

"Sleep deprived but steady," Rose whispered to Amaryllis as they walked to St. Michael's. Rose paused to wave to Mary, who was busily wiping the steamy front windows of her shop.

"You must meet Mary when we have time for me to introduce you. She makes the most delicious scone you've ever put in your mouth."

"Love that, Rose, but after the breakfast I tucked away this morning I doubt if I'll ever eat again."

"You earned it after your work last night. Your body was keeping up with your brain's hard drive. Which was on overtime. What will you tell the vicar?"

Amaryllis looked pensive then replied, "Well, all I can tell him is why the thefts are occurring. The vicar wants to know who the thieves are and that we do not know."

"Yet. I can tell him I have a few leads but I haven't made much progress in that direction. I don't believe we should tell the parishioners too much. Err on the side of caution, agree?"

"Absolutely. And I know Reverend Ellington feels the same way. His flock knows about the thefts and some think, as he does, that the stones are being sold to antique dealers. You know, 'old is gold' theory. I am willing to let folks just speculate until we can catch the thief. Or thieves."

The morning air was fresh and the two ladies walked in perfect harmony, enjoying the quiet of the early March morning. Birdsong broke over them as they approached the Village Green. Daffodils and pansies, wood anemones and even a few bluebells brightened unexpected corners along their walk: a patch of blue in front of the pub, a tiny window box of yellow at the village post office.

"Spring is definitely on its way," sighed Amaryllis. "I am sure Wynfield Farms is lovely now, also."

"Homesick, Amaryllis?" asked Rose, hopefully.

"No, no, just remembering. I did love my time in Virginia. You were the best part of it! But that was then and this is *now*. Of course, the downside of now means I have no home. I've left Australia, I'm here on temporary assignment. Where do I go from here?"

"Would you consider returning to Wynfield Farms? You'll always have a home there. Everyone would welcome you and your enthusiasm. And besides, Miss Moss is long gone."

"That despicable woman! What a harridan she was! And the new manager's name? You told me but I've forgotten."

"Mrs. Gallentine. Paula Gallentine."

"That's right. I'll think about Wynfield, Rose, I promise. But now, on to our assignment. I'll give this group a simple explanation of what has transpired and leave it to you to jolly them up with 'toad in a hole' or whatever is on their menu today."

"Suits me. Just hope they are a bit more receptive than the two characters I met yesterday."

The Reverend Coulton Ellington was standing by the lyche gate when Rose and Amaryllis approached the pathway to St. Michael's. He was having an animated conversation with Botts. The faithful caretaker was attired as usual in his double-breasted blue blazer and sported a jaunty blue cap on his head. Botts was leaning against the fence and nodding his head in agreement with the vicar.

Spotting the ladies, the vicar hailed them with a smile and "Welcome, friends. Doctor, I'm glad to see you and your magnificent pearls this morning."

"We got your note, vicar. What would you have us do?"

"We have about fifteen of our pensioners coming and I'd like . . . Oh, excuse me . . . you ladies do, of course, remember Mr. Botts, sexton extraordinaire?"

Botts doffed his hat.

"Of course. Good morning." chirped Rose. "A fine day to be outside."

"Botts and I were discussing a rotting timber on the porch. That can wait, Botts. Dr. Keynes-Livingston, could you say just a few words of explanation, well, *reassurance,* to the parishioners? I'll introduce you of course. They are all anxious about the thefts. And Mrs. McNess, I apologize again for imposing on your time but are you willing to help serve lunch to the group? We have some staff down there but—"

"Not near enough," growled Mr. Botts. "Folks nervous about the thievery. Don't go out."

"I'd consider it a privilege. Mr. Botts, could you accompany me to the Parish Hall? You've been here how long? Maybe twenty years? And I, a mere hour or so."

"More'n years I want to say."

Rose followed Willem Botts into the church and down the steps to the well-lit Parish Hall, leaving Amaryllis and Reverend Ellington discussing the status of the thefts and how much should be revealed to the assembled OAP's.

Rose asked, "Is your curate here today, Mr. Botts? I believe it's a Mr. Blakely."

"Only curate we have. No'm. Seems to be at meetings away. Vicar, he doesn't complain. Poor man has too much on his plate. Me'n Phyl, we do what we can to keep things runnin'. Not easy for a single man like vicar. Credit me with some sense: have my nephew comin' twice a week to help out. Yard work, most."

"St. Michael's is fortunate to have you, Mr. Botts. And your nephew if he is anything like you. Now, tell me where do I begin?"

At that moment a tiny dynamo sailed around the corner and promptly embraced Botts in a fierce hug. They both laughed and then the petite woman turned to Rose with, "The survey lady! Believe I met you and the other in vicar's office the cold afternoon."

"Right you are," replied Rose. "Survey or not, I'm here today to help with lunch. What's on the menu? I'm sure the pensioners are a hungry lot."

"Bangers and mash", replied Phyl Pickett. "Can't go wrong with that. Most of 'em don't eat proper. This'll stick to their ribs for a fortnight. Come on back and I'll kit you up with an apron."

⚬⚬⚬

Amaryllis, introduced by the vicar with emphasis on *Dr.* Keynes-Livingston, assured the group of fifteen older citizens that the investigation into thefts in East Plumley was proceeding with speed. No, she explained, the stones had not been recovered but she was certain they were not being sold.

Were the missing gravestones being copied or used as molds for other pieces? Hardly. No evidence whatsoever of that.

And what about the millstone? Would the town of East Plumley see that it was replaced? Dr. Keynes-Livingston assured the assembled that she would personally see that the town procured another millstone to be set in the very same spot as the missing one. There was much chatter among the group who were obviously curious about the mischief but even happier to be out and about on a fine spring day. With assurances from an American doctor that 'all will be well' in their churchyard and town, and a satisfying hot lunch in their body, why, indeed, would they not be happy?

⸎⊙᷎⊙⸎

"This has been the longest afternoon of my life, Rose. Give me test tubes and slides! Anything but fifteen OAP's grilling me not only about missing masonry but how would I cure sciatica? Or can one make plantar warts disappear completely? Whew! I'm hanging the 'DO NOT DISTURB' sign on the door and crawling under the covers for a few hours."

"You've earned it, Amaryllis. You did a superb job. And I know the vicar appreciated your help: he was positively beaming as you spoke."

"Was he?" Amaryllis asked shyly.

"Absolutely. He told me you'd agreed to speak to the congregation this coming Sunday. It's important to keep parishioners not only current but content."

"I'll prepare a longer spiel for Sunday and give them a bit about the algae and lichen. Do you think we are close to solving this, Rose?"

"Trust me. While you rest, I am taking myself to the pub. It's nearly four- thirty and, according to Deebs, the after-work crowd starts coming in soon. I'll do a lot of watching and listening. You get some sleep. If you feel like joining me later, I'll be there. The Rose and Thistle! Oh, I do love that name."

಄ⓞⓖ಄

Frances Keynes-Livingston untied her "working oxfords", wiggled her toes, sighed and curled up on her bed.

Ah, this is heavenly. Rose was spot-on: I am tired. Trying to make myself heard over the clamor of questions, all in a variety of accents, giving the responses they wanted to hear. Not necessarily the correct diagnosis. Serious chest pains! They should have gone directly to the Clinic, not wait for Senior Day for a free opinion. At least I gave them my honest opinion and not worthless pills.

Coulton was a huge help, though. So afraid I'd be overwhelmed by some of the town's biggest cry-babies. Little does he know the characters I've had to deal with in the field. He really is a sweetie.

I don't dare tell Rose that I'm meeting him at the vicarage tomorrow for breakfast. She'd never believe that we are planning to look over the St. Michael's census for the past century. I do so enjoy looking at the past to get a sense of where we are now. That will put Coulton and me on the same page, so to speak. I believe I will take a long hot bath now. I certainly want to rid myself of this clinical aroma I'm wearing. A hot bath should do the trick.

Chapter Twenty-One

Rose slipped into East Plumley's pub around five o'clock. She hoped to find a booth along the back wall, sit quietly and sip a half-pint of cider. She would read *Emma* and listen to the afternoon chatter. If invited, she would join in and then excuse herself to return to her book. Jane Austen was always a good plan.

"Evenin', Mrs. McNess! Deebs here. Glad to see you again. What'll you 'ave?"

"Deebs—I'm mighty glad to see you! This back booth is a perfect spot for reading. Let me see: pear cider? It's my favorite."

"Surely, Mam. Half or full?"

"Oh, I think a half will do, Deebs. And a bag of crisps with that."

I'm beginning to be a true Brit. Pub in the afternoon, cider and crisps. Deebs returned with her order, smiled broadly and left Rose to study her surroundings while ruffling the pages of her book.

Mostly male crowd stopping by after the five o'clock whistle, if there is still such a thing. I recognize a few faces from the other night - not many. Wait: the fellow that just came in, the one wearing the soiled jeans jacket. Is that a clasp on the jacket? Doesn't look like a button. Where is Deebs? He'll help me identify this fellow.

Rose's speculations were interrupted by the tall gray-haired gentleman who sauntered over to her table, bowed slightly and extended his hand.

"Rupert Pennington. I believe I met you with the vicar the other evening."

"Ah, good memory, Mr. Pennington. You did indeed. I am Mrs. McNess, from Virginia. Here with my friend on church survey business. The vicar has been so kind to us. Will you join me? I'm indulging in a glass of my favorite pear cider."

"And I come with Fuller's London Pride, the best in the county. Thank you, I'd be delighted. I still have a few minutes in my busy schedule."

"Please sit, Mr. Pennington. The vicar speaks so highly of you, I'm happy to have the chance to know you better."

"Coulton is prejudiced. And it's 'Rupert', please. We are fortunate in having someone of Coulton's caliber in the hamlet of East Plumley. He's a fine rector and well regarded. Excellent preacher and counselor. I suppose you've heard about the thefts in our churchyard? And the town. These incidents, I fear, are taking a heavy toll on Coulton. No businessman. Takes all kinds, of course. Myself, business is in my blood. That's what it's all about. These incidents though, never had anything like it before in East Plumley."

So the vicar is 'no businessman' but he is! What ego.

"Oh, yes, we've heard about the mischief. And we are very sympathetic. My associate, Dr. Keynes-Livingston, has been most helpful in examining the specific aspects of the church yard. But tell me, would you happen to know the young man in the jeans jacket? He's over to the left, at the table with two older fellows. Could I have seen him in one of the shops along the High?"

Rupert Pennington turned to look at the door and in doing so glimpsed the young man Rose was eager to identify.

Scowling, he replied to Rose, "Trevor Botts, Willem Botts' nephew. Botts does all he can to keep the fellow out of trouble, but Botts is nearly seventy if he's a day, and just too old, really, to have much of an influence on him. Old Botts has taken him on at St. Michael's to help with grounds. How long he'll last is anyone's guess."

"Thank you. Perhaps I may have caught a glimpse of him at St. Michael's. He does look vaguely familiar, but then I've met so many folks here in East Plumley. Now, tell me about your work, Mr. Pennington: I'm a good listener."

"I fear I'm of little interest, Mrs. McNess. Other than being a life-long resident of East Plumley and a life member of St. Michael's, I have no claim to fame"

"You are too modest. Didn't I hear you were town solicitor? Which means you keep track of all deeds, debts and deaths in East Plumley. I believe everyone's profession is important and that certainly applies to yours."

"Are all Virginians so flattering, Mrs. McNess? I simply do my job and enjoy what I am doing. My wife and I live quietly. No children. Naturally I have had a few thoughts about running for higher office, but the timing's not been right. Besides, hardly pays to be a public official. No gain. Good friends such as the Vicar make my life infinitely more pleasant. That's why this nasty business of the thefts has me worried. Coulton is taking it personally. Damnedest thing that's ever happened here."

"I don't want to be a 'Nosey Parker', but between the two of us, do you have any suspicions? While working on my survey I've met a few East Plumley residents. Everyone seems to have a different notion but no real clues."

"Ms. McNess, obviously I must choose my words very carefully. But talking as we are, friend to friend-if I may presume upon a new friendship— I have doubts about Coulton's new curate."

"I appreciate your trust in me, Mr. Pennington. Tell me, what *are* your doubts?"

"The fellow's never here! When Coulton looks for assistance with his outreach programs Blakely has disappeared. When he does return, chewing on his strange nuts and berries, he's too shy to look one in the eye."

"You make him sound 'curiouser and curiouser'! Where was Blakely prior to his assignment?"

"New Guinea. Two years in the jungle. Teaching English to the natives. When he landed back in England he needed a parish and I guess Coulton felt sorry for the bloke. Our last curate had just left and it was a matter of Blakely being in the right spot at the right time. As a virtual stranger in town, he could be in on any number of deals, and none of us would be the wiser."

Deals? thought Rose. Mr. Pennington, you are the only one talking about deals.

"Perhaps he's just shy and uncomfortable after being the 'Big Man' for two years. Doesn't know how to well, *relate,* to ordinary mortals in a small English village. Ever try talking one-on-one with the fellow?"

Rose was not about to admit to Mr. Pennington that Amaryllis had experienced the same thing during her meeting with Blakely.

"No, I confess I should have. I'll force myself to try. No, I *will* try. For Coulton's sake. Oh, best sign my chit before Deebs chases me out! There— would you be so kind, madam, as to see that Deebs gets this when he returns?"

Smiling at Rose, Rupert Pennington replaced his blue pen in the inner pocket of his jacket and said, "But now I must be off. Wife will be watching the clock. A delightful visit, Mrs. McNess. Surely we'll see each other again? St. Michael's this Sunday, if not before."

"It has been mutually delightful, Mr. Pennington. Indeed, we'll see you on Sunday."

Golly. Never would have pegged Mr. Pennington as a 'talker'. That man is not who he pretends to be. Why did I have this feeling during our entire conversation that a black cloud hovered over me? A creepy premonition that I couldn't shake. Strange, I get these vibrations so rarely that I can remember each and every one. It's as if a malevolent force is about to leap out and obliterate every rational thought I may have in my head.

Rose sat still as a stone. She trembled as she fingered her class of cider. I'm missing something. I certainly don't want to share this with Amaryllis. I'm sure she already thinks I am just dithering and have gone 'round the bend.

Rupert Elwood Pennington paused as he left the pub, stepping to one side as he saw Mr. Gresham sauntering toward him with a four o'clock smile on his face.

"Ah, Gresham. I assure you that I have left adequate ale for your afternoon refreshment. Does a man good to look forward, eh?"

"'Evenin', sire. Yessiree. Busy day in m'shop. Body cryin' out for a sip o' somethin' Rose-like."

"Glad to know you are prospering, Mr. Gresham. Have a good one!" Gresham tipped his cap, removed it, and entered The Rose, wondering what had prompted the normally stuffed-shirt Pennington's jovial outburst.

Rupert Pennington was feeling anything but jovial. He walked toward the Green, hoping that Gresham would be the last of his encounters this afternoon.

Damn and blast these visitors of Ellington's. No pulling the wool over my eyes: they are on to something more than a survey. One of my sheep has been careless. Old Botts? Certainly not Botts: paid him a king's ransom last week. More than he deserved because I know young Trevor is doing all the lifting. Trevor? Drink making him careless? I'll deal with that at the warehouse. Warehouse crew? Dumb as ten dead oxen. Keep moving my boxes of 'grain' to the East, that's all I ask. Post Office? Nah, all the money comes in normal business papers. Old Norm wouldn't question the Town Solicitor, 'specially since I have my own letter box. Town Solicitor has to have some perks.

Damned, not enough perks. I'm bigger than this. I'll show them. I *will* show them. Timing has got to be just right: a few more months, say, six, and then I'll have enough money to ease out of this dumpy village. And a dumpy marriage . . . which I should face in another ten minutes or so. Sheila still expects the dutiful hubby home by five. But at least she doesn't question all my evening meetings . . . Ah—wouldn't it just be grand to turn around and join old Gresham for another pint at The Rose?

Chapter Twenty-Two

"Another, Ma'am?"

Deebs appeared at Rose's booth, tray in hand and eager to refill her order.

"Oh, Deebs. Yes, please. Another pear cider; it is delicious. But wait a sec, please, if may ask you something. Between us, if you don't mind."

Deebs leaned closer, eyes wide. "Of course, Ma'am."

"The fellow in the corner, the one with the jeans jacket: is he really Willem Botts' nephew? I've met Mr. Botts and this young man bears no resemblance at all."

"That's 'Trouble Botts' all right. 'Trouble's' what we call 'em. Real name is Trevor. The dust up here the other night? 'Twas 'Trouble'. Don't really want 'em and his pals in The Rose but what can you do? 'E's not causin' ruckus now, but soon as he gets too big for 'is britches, you can be sure Willis has 'em out of here."

"Willis? Oh, the Rose's owner."

"That's correct, Ma'am. He don't put up with any mischief in The Rose."

"Thank you, Deebs. I was just curious. He bears no re-semblance to his uncle. And don't forget my cider, please."

Two rather interesting descriptions of Trevor Botts. If I could just wiggle closer to get a really good look at that jacket, I might convince myself I had the thief. Perhaps he'll toss it over the chair. I could steal a peek as I walked by. Oh, for heavens' sake: look who just walked through the blue door.

Stewart Blakely made his way through the now-crowded pub and sat at a table a short distance from Rose's booth. Im-pulsively, Rose walked over to stand beside his table.

"Mr. Blakely. Twice in two days! How could I be so lucky?"

Mr. Blakely rose, his face rapidly turning scarlet. "I, I am sorry I missed you at St. Michael's this morning. Had a meet-ing in Ely that I couldn't skip, Did the vicar explain?"

"As a matter of fact, he did not. I met the entire staff but you were among the missing."

"Please, sit here, Mrs....I'm sorry, I'm terrible at names."

"McNess. Mrs. Rose McNess. And I will sit a moment, thank you."

"I'm expecting my friends soon, but they aren't always on time so we can talk until they arrive."

"Your friends? The same ones we saw at **BIRYANI** last evening?"

"The same. They're refugees. Syrian refugees."

"And you?"

"I'm teaching them English, Mrs. McNess. Rather, *at-tempting* to teach them. I have a syllabus but I'm not that good. And they are desperate to learn our language. Absolutely desperate."

Rose, chastened because of the prior thoughts she and Amaryllis had harbored about Mr. Blakely, sank back into her chair.

"What can I do to help? I've worked with the ESL program in the States. It works, it really does! Everything takes time, Mr. Blakely. If you have the stamina to tough it out and your students are willing to study, you'll be amazed at the progress they'll make. I promise."

"Oh, they're willing to study. Time is our problem. I'm sure the vicar thinks I am goofing off because I leave so often. But the fellows' jobs are irregular and I have to juggle schedules to arrange our meetings. Last night was their first meal in a *real* restaurant. I made them read the menus to me. I wish you could have heard *that*."

"May I make a suggestion, Mr. Blakely?"

"Please. I need all the help I can get."

"Confide in Reverend Ellington. He would much rather know *where* you are and *what* you are doing than wonder when you just take off into the blue—"

"Of course, you're right. I've neglected him, Mrs. McNess. I've neglected St. Michael's, the congregation—"

"Just think of it as a temporary lapse, Mr. Blakely. Now, in case your fellows suddenly appear, I'll slip back to my seat. I'm here to study, anyway. And thank you for telling me what you are doing. It is a wonderful service."

"Mrs. McNess?"

"Yes, Mr. Blakely?"

"Uh, um, well, I wonder if you have time, before the lads come, uh, could you spare a few minutes?"

"Of course, Mr. Blakely. Let me grab my cider and **Emma**. One minute."

Rose returned after collecting both items, wondering what this shy young man had on his mind. "Now Mr. Blakely, how can I be of service? I'm a good listener."

The curate blushed, his face growing redder by the minute. "Please, its Stewart. I'm still wrestling with being Mr. Blakely. I'd so appreciate your calling me 'Stewart'."

"Stewart it is then. What were you called at your last post? Did I hear you were in New Guinea?"

"Big Tosh. Don't ask me how they came up with that. Big Tosh or just Tosh for the last two years. But please, Stewart if you don't mind."

"Of course. Now, to business. What do you have on your mind? Rather, to the point, why did you wish to speak with me?"

"It's a delicate matter Mrs. McNess. But you being a married lady and all…"

"A widowed lady, Stewart, and an older widowed lady at that. But continue."

"Right. One of my chaps wants to get married. I am trying to persuade Amar to wait until he passes the literacy test.

He insists that the test does not matter. He says he's in love and wants to marry in June."

"A love story—I'm so glad you have spoken to me, Stewart."

"Yes, and it is a love story. Amar's intended is also Syrian, but she's lived here almost five years. Her English is exceptional. She has a good job, and besides that, she is beautiful. Her name is Avi."

"Why are you discouraging him? Didn't you say the young men had jobs?"

"Oh, they have decent well-paying work, Mrs. McNess. But they'll have even better jobs when they are fluent in English. I just feel Amar's wife will have more respect for him if he passes his fluency test before he marries. Let's say, well, they'll be entering matrimony as equals."

"Stewart, I think you are absolutely right. Obviously you have a clear grasp of human nature, and the consequences of matrimony. But how in the world can I help?"

Mr. Blakely's face registered his relief. "Oh, Mrs. McNess, thank you for understanding. Right now the first thing you can do is speak to Amar when he comes in this afternoon. I'll handle introductions, so no worries there. If that goes well, would you be willing to meet with Avi, his intended? I could set that up."

"I cannot meet Amar this afternoon, Stewart. Let's arrange to meet tomorrow morning. I'll go with you to Amar and talk, then meet with Avi."

"They both live in Swaffham. I'll be happy to arrange this and I'll be happy to drive as well."

"Lovely. I'm sure I can manage a short expedition to Swaffham in the morning. You set it up, Stewart. It will be my pleasure to chat with Avi and Amar. Oh, here come your students. Stewart, it's your show."

Rose picked up her book, patted Stewart Blakely on the arm, and smiled at Stewart's two pupils as they made their way to his table.

Golly! I was sure Blakely was our Number One suspect. As did Amaryllis, particularly after last evening's meeting. How could we have been so wrong? Oh golly! Now I'm playing Cupid while trying to figure out Pennington. That pen he used to sign his chit…

Chapter Twenty-Three

Rose knocked on Amaryllis' closed door, hoping that her partner in crime was not still resting.

"Rose? Back so soon? Come in. I'm just going over my notebook. I've so many species of lichen listed that I can hardly keep them straight in my head…"

"Amaryllis, listen!"

"Whoa, Rose. You look as if you had uncovered something big. Tell me."

"I'm trying. I cannot prove it—yet—but I think your Roalla—Rosie—is the reason for all the thefts!"

"That common lichen…?"

"Yes, you said it was a component of ink. It's ink that the thugs are desperate to manufacture. Lots and lots of ink! And where do they get the ingredient for this ink? Right here in East Plumley!"

"What?"

"Just listen. My seatmate flying over last week had a blue pen that he used in his business. I witnessed how the ink appeared on paper: practically *invisible* until one shifted the paper a certain way. A container could be labeled anything, with the *actual* contents written elsewhere with *this* ink. Think of what that could do with boxes innocently labelled dog food, salt, peas. Recipients could pick these up and actually be taking delivery of ammunition or drugs. Particularly useful in the drug trade I would imagine—"

"Rose, that is brilliant. Meanwhile, Cambridge has gotten back to me and confirmed my findings. This particular alga has a low life span *until* it is combined with a stronger partner. Then it radiates almost indefinitely. You've made a miraculous discovery. How in the world did you make the connection?"

"Well, Mr. Rupert Pennington stopped by for a chat. He's quite the 'wheeler dealer' and proud of it. He signed his bar chit with a blue pen that was identical to one I had seen before. It was surreal, Amaryllis, but in my mind's eye I could see my seatmate writing furiously. I am sure Pennington has the identical pen capable of using the invisible ink."

Then Rose grew somber for a moment. She briefly told Amaryllis of her conversation with Stewart Blakely; having decided that it was time for the two of them to share the guilt they had harbored toward the curate.

"The young man is lonely, Amaryllis. His students are his friends and his main focus. I believe I helped put him on the path to being a real help to the vicar. And…" Rose hesitated.

Will Amaryllis think I am becoming more of a busy-body than I already am?

"And *what*, Rose? You have more on your mind than a blue pen and Mr. Blakely. As if that is not enough. I repeat, and *what?*"

"Don't be touchy. I have agreed to help him with a situation. A situation of romance."

"I knew it! Rose McNess, my soft-hearted friend who finds love in bloom anywhere on the planet. Who's the object of your affection this time, Cupid?"

Rose smiled. She ignored her friend's caustic humor and said. "Amaryllis, please cut the sarcasm. Think of this as a good deed I happen to be quite capable of handling. I'm going to Swaffham in the morning to consult with the lovelorn, one of Blakely's students."

"As if we didn't have enough mystery on our hands, LOVE rears its head. Or heart. Oh, Rose, darling, solve away in Swaffham, because I think you've solved our mystery of the lichen. I'll call Cambridge in the morning and run the ink theory by them. Now we've got two parts of this puzzle: the *why* of the thefts and the *raison d'etre*. But who? Or whom? Any theories there, Sherlock? Or should I say, Cupid?"

"As a matter of fact, I do. Enough theories to make me want to ring the town constable and have them meet us at St. Michael's on Sunday."

"Go on. We've scratched Mr. Blakely from the list so—"

"Remember the broken clasp I brought back the other day? We decided that it might be a clue. Well, I am not pointing fingers yet, but I saw someone in the pub this evening that wore a jacket *with* clasps. I couldn't get close enough to see if one was broken but I did find out the identity of the jacket's owner."

"Rose, I am almost afraid to ask. Tell me!"

"Sadly, Willem Botts' nephew. The fellow causing the 'dust up' our first night at the pub. Deebs called him 'Trouble' Botts. You remember the Vicar telling us about his unfortunate background, and how his uncle had taken him on at the church to do some work around the place. Miss Tilly at AGELESS ANTIQUES had some doubts about him. 'Trouble' or Trevor has immediate access to all of the tombstones, night or day. If only we could catch him in the act."

"We might stay here for weeks and never see that. He must be stopped."

"The one way to stop him is to cut off his supply of ready money. Trevor is no fool: he's collecting cold, hard cash for each artifact he delivers."

"And do you have any suspects in that department, Rose?"

"The Town Solicitor: Reverend Coulton Ellington's trusted friend, Rupert Pennington. He's the man with the blue pen."

"Rose—I can't believe you! He's practically a pillar of the community. What proof do you have?"

"At the present, only my intuition and the pen. After my unexpected and lengthy conversation with Mr. Pennington, I do not think he is willing to face the embarrassment of a long trial or imprisonment. Once arrested, he will plead not guilty or temporary insanity or another equally lame excuse. When Trevor starts telling his story and revealing the cash he has received over the past month, who will get the sympathy? And the conviction? Yes, Amaryllis, its only on the basis of my intuition but I think we call the constables and tell them to be at St. Michael's on Sunday."

"But you didn't see money change hands or see anything specific."

"You'll have to trust me, Amaryllis. Mr. Pennington *has* the funds. He is a vain ambitious man, and he sees himself as *more* than a solicitor."

"I trust your judgment, Rose. I've been working on my remarks for Sunday and I'll be purposely vague on details. I'll just reassure the crowd that the entire churchyard is not disappearing. You know that Willem will be on hand, and probably Mr. Pennington. And perhaps what's his name, also. What did you say they call him?"

"'Trouble'. Deebs called him 'Trouble' and I'm sticking with that. Now, will you put the number for the Swaffham constabulary in your phone? We need to be alert and I need to be polishing my "advice to the lovelorn" skills if I am to help the curate."

Chapter Twenty-Four

A late night phone call sealed Rose and Blakely's meeting at nine o'clock the next morning for their rendezvous in Swaffham. The curate was as good as his word, arriving at the Arms on the dot of nine.

Rose waved to Giles as she left, calling "Off to Swaffham!", knowing full well the old warrior would be intrigued by her defection, and would undoubtedly interrogate Amaryllis when she appeared for breakfast.

"Oh, I hope so!" Rose giggled as she sailed out the door.

Settled in Stewart's small sedan, Rose was instantly comfortable with the young man. The car reminded Rose of the many vehicles her children and grandchildren had driven through the years. She'd often been their passenger on the way to college, to far-flung jobs, even to weddings. Seats slightly frayed, backseat piled with books and detritus of life. Even the old car *smell* was familiar.

"Did you have much trouble persuading Amar to let us speak with his intended?"

"Are you asking if I twisted his arm?" smiled Blakely, glancing at Rose as he navigated the narrow East Plumley streets.

"No, just wondering about your powers of persuasion."

"I told Amar that you were the most sensible woman I knew. Since he is rather dependent upon me for advancing his cause in this situation, he agreed immediately."

"Good. It's a fine morning for a drive. I think that is a good omen for our mission."

"Your mission, Mrs. McNess. I am merely the chauffer."

Rose smiled, "Fine, I'll just take this opportunity to learn a bit more about my chauffer. Are you from East Anglia, Stewart?"

"Oh, no, Mrs. McNess. I hate the flatness of all this. I was born and raised in Oxfordshire."

"So you are an Oxford man, I take it?"

"No Ma'am. Cambridge. My dad's a don at Oxford and we thought it best to put a little distance."

"I can appreciate that Stewart, but I hope you have good relations with your family."

"Indeed. See them every month or so. I like East Plumley, but I miss the hills, and I have to admit the town is a little slow after the bustle of Oxford."

"There is nothing like a university town," agreed Rose. "East Plumley may be a bit quiet after Oxford and Cambridge, but you managed to find good causes to pursue. You have taken on quite a challenge with your students. Tell me, since I am being nosey, do you get along with the vicar?"

"Indeed! Reverend Ellington is a rare one. I'm incredibly fortunate. He has a wry sense of humor. Oh yes, he is a grand fellow. And he's captain of East Plumley's cricket club. Did you know that?"

Rose shook her head. No, she knew nothing of the vicar's athletic prowess, but Rose wondered if Amaryllis had enjoyed any of the vicar's wry humor during her tête-à-têtes at St. Michael's.

"We are now entering Swaffham, Mrs. McNess. And let's see, Avi and Amar are waiting for us in the tea shoppe on Ledford Street. Hmmmm…."

Stewart Blakely continued down one winding street after another and finally pulled to the curb on what looked like Swaffham's 'high street'. Rose glanced at the grim buildings and immediately decided that this town did not have the charm of East Plumley.

Stewart led the way as they walked a short distance before entering the *Four Lads' Tea Shoppe*. Avi and Amar huddled in deep conversation at a table near the back of the cheerless room.

Rose looked around, hoping that *The Four Lads* had decent tea because it had little else going for it.

Amar stood immediately, a smile breaking across his face. The lovely Avi sat demurely, smiling even as a few tears streaked her face. The black hijab pulled severely over her hair merely highlighted beautiful brown eyes.

"Avi, Amar, meet my friend Mrs. McNess, from Virginia, in the United States. Vir-gin-ia. As I told Amar, she is a very wise person. I hope you will listen to her and take her words to heart. It is indeed matters of the heart that concern us today."

Rose blushed—*wise person!* Her pride in Curate Blakely grew immensely as he initiated what might turn out to be a very prickly conversation.

She began, "Avi, Amar, may I call you by your given names?" A nod from both. Rose continued, "I am here to wish you well on your journey as one – not two people. Marriage means two become one equal. It is a sharing of all matters of the heart, health, home, and with more difficulty, finance. No matter what dreams or hopes one has, equality in stature and self-worth is essential."

Avi's tears had stopped and the couple's eyes were riveted upon Rose. Both were serious, attentive and looked as if they were clinging to Rose's every word.

"Avi, I understand that your language skills are exceptional. How long have you been in the UK—two years?"

"Five. I finished Ely night college two years ago."

"Wonderful! And you, Amar: I know you are Mr. Blakely's prize student. How well are you getting along with the language?"

"Not as well as Avi! I work hard…."

"Oh, he does, Mrs. McNess," broke in Mr. Blakely. "He *is* my prize student. But we simply have not been at it as long as Avi."

"I understand," nodded Rose. "Amar, aside from the fact that you are clearly besotted with Avi, what is the rush to get married in June? A mere three months away."

"Love," stated Amar, with no hesitation, He clasped Avi's hands tightly and looked into her eyes.

"I can understand that," Rose said softly. "But I also know how difficult it is for immigrants in the UK. I am no expert, but I know you are expected to assimilate quickly, learn the new ways, so unlike the Syrian life you've left behind. Avi, do you understand what I mean about equals?"

"I do, Mrs. Rose."

"Would you like to begin married life with a husband who understands and speaks the language as well as yourself? Whom you can send to the green grocer with a list of food—words he knows— without your having to translate his every purchase? Who, when the time comes, *and it will,* that there is a new member entering your family, he will be able to talk to the midwife or call hospital? Will he know about taking you to the mosque?"

The couple huddled and whispered softly to each other as Rose and Stewart deliberately focused their attention on the menu board on the opposite wall.

Amar was the first to speak. He looked at Avi as he spoke. "Mrs. McNess, Avi says you are wise, and correct. I will wait—I wish to make Avi proud. We will marry in Autumn, when the moon cycle is upon us."

"Oh, Amar you are wise as well. And Avi, you are a fortunate young woman to have a man as perceptive as Amar. Congratulations! And please no tears, Avi, or you will have this old lady bawling in her tea cup."

Everyone laughed, and Stewart Blakely stood, a wide grin crossing his face. "I say, I think this calls for another cuppa and a slice of this seed cake they feature today. My treat! Everyone agree?"

The foursome celebrated their decision with tea and cake and peals of laughter as Rose struggled to learn their language and they, hers.

When Stewart Blakely returned Rose to the Plumley Arms that afternoon, he turned to her and said simply, "Mrs. McNess, today I have learned more about human nature— from you— than in all my years at Cambridge or New Guinea. Thank you, thank you."

When Rose returned to the suite, Amaryllis was at the desk, engrossed in her slides. Looking up she asked, "Well, Cupid, how did it go?"

"I'll just say *mission accomplished!*"

Amaryllis smiled benignly. No need to tell Rose of my morning. Breakfast . . .was divine! Coulton had prepared a more-than-decent omelet, crisp bacon, croissants from Mary's, and tea just the way I like it: hot, hot, hot. No need to mention, either, that the vicar, minus his collar, in his home, was warm and chatty, considerate and charming. A delightful suitor. Was I a wanton woman? No, no just an appreciative listener. A leaner-on-the-shoulder sort of woman. Oh Rose, what have I gotten us into in East Plumley?

Chapter Twenty-Five

Rose and Amaryllis retired early. Each was experiencing a dizzying whirl of emotions, not only from what had happened but what they feared would happen.

Amaryllis silently rehearsed her brief address to the parishioners of St. Michael's. I will speak as a member of a worldwide church survey team that has spent these days perusing St. Michael's history and property.

Then I'll continue, with enthusiasm, but certainly referring to my notes. If the good folks of East Plumley see me as a scientist, then they shall be expecting a rather scholarly approach.

"What a jewel you have here in East Plumley! Sadly, the disappearance of three century-old gravestones from the churchyard has been highly irregular and upsetting, not only for the vicar but also for you, the St. Michael's family. As a scientist, I can only guess that the stones have been removed because of the lichen on the stones. Yes, the ordinary lichen contains a chemical substance that is needed in research."

I'll be purposely vague about what that could be, how we are working to recover the stones if at all possible, etc., etc., and what a delight it has been to be a guest of the parish. There! I do not want to talk more than 3-4 minutes. And I cannot show too much exuberance for my subject. There will be no time for questions as Coulton said his sermon would follow immediately. Most satisfactory!

Rose lay in bed reflecting on events of the past few several days.

I really am grateful that Mr. Blakely—Stewart—is not a suspect. He needs a shot of confidence if he is to be of any help to Reverend Ellington. But what about Botts' nephew? Very sad situation but also very shady. And the town solicitor, the respected Mr. Pennington? Have I thought all this out properly? I cannot accuse Trevor Botts of theft on the basis of a missing jacket clasp. Of course I have the clasp and if he should happen to wear the jacket in the morning…no, I don't see that happening. Not in a million years. He probably won't even show up. And no one wants to break the news to old Botts. It will shatter the man. His own nephew stealing from St. Michael's. Why, Mr. Botts is practically a legend in East Plumley, not to mention St. Michael's. And how will my revelation about Mr. Pennington affect the vicar? How could the vicar not sense his obsequiousness? His intense interest in the missing headstones? The vicar counted Pennington not only as a friend but also as a man with the best interests of St. Michael's at heart.

Such thoughts kept the two sleuths tossing and turning until the wee hours when they finally closed uneasy eyes.

Morning came and the ladies dressed with care and a certain piquancy to bolster their spirits. They enjoyed a full English breakfast at The Arms and were soon on their way to St. Michael's for the ten o'clock service.

"Nervous, Amaryllis?"

"Heavens, no. Just eager to get on with this. Does my skirt look wrinkled? And have you thought how we'll tell the vicar about the Botts' fellow? His name again?"

"What do you think kept *me* awake until midnight? His name is Trevor. Trevor or Trouble Botts. And no, your skirt does not look wrinkled. Keep moving Amaryllis, it's half past nine."

"And your plan, Rose? I am paying attention as I walk. Fast enough for you?"

"Perfect. I've thought it out in detail but that doesn't necessarily mean it will go as planned. I shall ask the vicar to convene a meeting of the five of us: you, me, Rupert Pennington, Botts and the vicar. I'll suggest the office for privacy. Then we will spell out our suspicions, reveal that constables have been notified, and ask Botts for help in locating Trevor. I just know that fellow will not darken the church doors this morning. I am counting on Reverend Ellington for moral support, even if he may be too stunned to speak."

"Brilliant, Rose! I agree with your every word. I will back you up and ask pertinent questions at the proper times."

The pair was approaching the lyche gate when Rose suddenly grabbed Amaryllis' sleeve and whispered, "Look. There." She pointed to the apse of the church.

"What? I was lost in thought."

"A flash of blue. Botts' blazer. I know he saw us. That means he will definitely be on hand this morning. Maybe our talk with him won't be as difficult as we fear."

"Are you sure it was Mr. Botts, Rose? Could he see us from the churchyard? Perhaps he was finishing a chore. Sextons have a busy time on Sunday mornings."

"Amaryllis, he saw us approaching and deliberately ducked behind the church. I recognized the blue of his old blazer. Remember the vicar said he wore it daily, rain or shine? It was definitely Botts and he did *not* want to be seen."

They walked on, paused at the entrance to St. Michael's and nodded to many of the parishioners, who smiled at them. The 'church survey' by two American visitors had obviously been well advertised among the members.

Mr. Denison smiled and bobbed as he greeted Rose, as did Mr. Gresham from the hardware shop. (*And isn't he all spiffed up today!*)

Rose did not see Mimslyn Welford among those gathered at the porch, and wondered if she had finished mutilating the poor tree.

"Why, good morning Mary, I'm still remembering your scones."

"Hoping you'll be back. Good to gab with ya. 'Morrow morning, rum and raisin!" Mary smiled as she winked at Rose, knowing that she might entice the American lady to join her once again.

Miss Tilly appeared at Rose's elbow. She was immaculate in black. The sparkling netting of her jaunty flycatcher chapeau was matched by the sheen of her red hair and wide smile.

"Rose, is your new friend Celeste here? I'm dying to catch a glimpse of her."

"I don't see her, Amaryllis. If she's here, I'll introduce her after the service. I'll take a seat on the aisle, near the front. A bit to the side of the pulpit. I don't want to look as if I am staring at you the entire time. Good luck, dear!"

Amaryllis waited at the rear of the nave. Sunlight poured through the narrow windows and diamonds of blues and reds danced over the heads of the congregation. The crucifer, the acolytes, and eight-member choir processed by her. Mr. Blakely and Reverend Ellington waved her in front of them in the march as the organist pounded out William Blake's appropriately rousing *Jerusalem.*

"Is there any hymn more English or stirring," thought Rose.

Prayers, the Creed, responses went as well as they had done for the past two hundred-plus years at St. Michael's. Rose felt comfortable in the Church of England service.

She was quietly reflecting on her impressions of East Plumley when Reverend Ellington stood to introduce "Dr. Keynes-Livingston, a member of a church survey team from the States. She has uncovered some facts we should acknowledge about our beloved St. Michael's. I ask you to give a warm and attentive welcome to Dr. Keynes-Livingston."

Polite applause preceded Amaryllis as she stepped to the lectern and smiled at the congregation. Rose smiled also, proud of her accomplished friend. As she beamed at Amaryllis, Rose happened to glance upward at the heavy reticulated bonnet above the lectern. It was beginning to sway!

Am I imagining this? The cord on the bonnet!

"Amaryllis! Move! Now!" Shouting, Rose leaped from the pew and hurled herself up the altar steps, tackling Amaryllis in her mid-section and throwing both of them down in a tangled heap at the feet of the stately Bishop's Chair. Seconds later the bonnet crashed down on the lectern: a direct hit that shattered each piece of church property into large, jagged spears of ancient chestnut. Chaos erupted!

Centuries of dust motes continued to rise, swirl and fall for what seemed like an eternity, wreathing the scene in a miasma of grime and splinters. The hanging end of the bonnet tether swayed, spun, unraveled. In relating the story later, Mr. Gresham would recall that the end of the cord resembled nothing so much as a chewed up, spit-out old cigar.

The congregation, stunned, confused, and mute, for a second was in disbelief. As they slowly comprehended what they had just witnessed, there were wails and shouts as every man and woman stood and began to press forward for a closer look at the calamity.

"Aged old thing, what a pity it broke today."

"Those poor women, someone call the doctor…"

"Guess the budget'll have to stretch for 'nother bonnet. Always been part of St. Michael's."

"Anyone have the doctor on their mobile?"

"That spry Mrs. McNess! Did you see her race up those steps?"

"She's a proper one alright. Should have seen her in m'store. Knew more about tools than most men," quipped Mr. Gresham.

"And veggies," chimed in Mr. Meekins. "Right proper lady. Terrible shame this happened to a visitor from the US. Terrible 'appen to any old soul."

Reverend Ellington, pale and shaken, was trying to keep a semblance of order and at the same time tend to the two women on the altar floor.

Finally regaining his composure and voice, he quickly dismissed the congregation.

"Mr. Blakeley will accompany you to the Parish Hall. Please gather for fellowship and prayers for the well-being of our two distinguished visitors. Mr. Blakely…"

Rose saw Stewart Blakely, hand raised, half-smile on his pale face, waving the assembled throng through the door to the Parish Hall. Celeste, a vision today in a voluminous violet frock, was urging the stragglers along.

"Rose darling! You saved my life! Look at the girth of that bonnet: solid chestnut, two-hundred plus years. I would have been *flattened.* Did I say something *incendiary* that caused the velvet to disintegrate?"

"I am so glad you can speak, Amaryllis. I could have knocked the wind out of you permanently."

"Almost, but . . . not . . . quite . . . permanently."

"Amaryllis, there are no jagged edges to indicate a slow dissolution of the antique roping. If you'd had an 'incendiary' remark in your head, it's still there. The bonnet's cord had clearly been cut near the ceiling. *Neatly* cut, I might add."

Having discharged the remnants of his congregation to the Parish Hall, Reverend Ellington hurried to the two women on the altar floor. He turned to Amaryllis, now sitting upright, long legs stretched in front of her.

"My dear Doctor, this is a disaster. You were almost killed in this accident. I am, well, without words. I don't know what to say to you, or how to apologize properly. We must get you to hospital. I insist on it."

By this time Rose had managed to stand. She smoothed her skirt and jacket and then spoke calmly. "Vicar, this was no accident. Dr. Keynes-Livingston and I know who has been stealing the headstones, and she – the good doctor– was going to talk about that this morning. The perpetrator sensed that we were on to him, or them, and was going to make sure that my friend never opened her mouth. Simply put, this is a case of attempted murder."

"Murder! Dear Lord! That is frightful! I . . . I'm in disbelief. An accusation like that here, in St. Michael's . . . I can barely speak. Are you quite certain of your facts, Mrs. McNess?"

Amaryllis, now sprawled in the Bishop's Chair, spoke. "Tell him of our suspects, Rose. I'm too shaken to speak properly."

"Not suspects: the culprit. You have only one person in the parish with access to a ladder tall enough to reach the top of the bonnet cord. One person who knew the strength of the cord and if it would hang just long enough for Frances – Dr. Keynes-Livingston – to position herself under it. Had you lingered ten seconds longer with your introduction, Vicar, you, not Frances, would have been the victim."

"But who, Mrs. McNess?"

"Sadly, the villain in this case is none other than Mr. Willem Botts."

"Rose!"

"Botts?"

"Yes. I worked that out during the morning prayers. Botts and his nephew are in on this operation together."

"This is impossible to believe, Mrs. McNess. Was Botts in church today? He never *misses* early service on Sunday."

"Oh, he was here. I did not see him after I joined the congregation, but I doubt if he's far away. I'll let you call the constable to bring him in for questioning. Somehow I think his conscience might be bothering him right about now."

"That's not what is bothering me," squeaked Amaryllis. "Rose, you tackled me. I ache in my midsection as if I'd had two or three Heimlich maneuvers. Vicar, could we be excused to retreat to The Arms? I promise to return tomorrow and explain the *why* of this mystery."

"Indeed, indeed, ladies, how thoughtless of me not to think of your condition. But I do think you should go to hospital."

"Absolutely not! All I need is a bit of rest and a very large dram of brandy."

"If you insist, my dear. I'll go find Rupert Pennington to drive you to *The Arms*. I'm sure he's downstairs. If you'll wait just a moment—"

Rose and Amaryllis exchanged looks before Rose called, "Vicar! Please! Wait!"

The vicar turned and looked at Rose with a quizzical expression. "I'm sure he will be happy to run you to the Arms."

Rose put her hand on the vicar's arm and spoke softly, "I'm afraid there is more to this story. Your friend Rupert Pennington has been deceiving you. He's as mixed up in this disaster as Botts and his nephew. Mr. Pennington is not downstairs with the congregation. If I am not mistaken, I saw Mr. Pennington leave by the side entrance when Amaryllis was catching her breath. The Swaffham constables will be taking him in shortly. Now, Amaryllis, let me find us a ride and we'll be off."

Chapter Twenty-Six

"Rose, I am perfectly capable of walking back to the Arms. Slowly. I *am* able to operate on my own steam. No ride, please. I do not want to answer all the inevitable questions. Let's just move on quietly. Please."

"Are you sure? And if the answer is 'yes', there is one more thing we must do before leaving St. Michael's this morning."

"And that is?"

"Look for Trevor Botts. We have almost overlooked him in all the hoopla over the accident. But I have a feeling he's still hanging around the churchyard. Maybe that is why Botts was heading there when we came in this morning. Remember, I pointed out Botts' blue blazer?"

"Vaguely. I didn't see the patch of blue but obviously you did. Yes, now I recall your telling me. But why would Trouble be here early on a Sunday morning when members surely would spot him if he decided to wander through the churchyard?"

"I know it doesn't make sense, but *nothing* else does either! I am going to look in the churchyard. Coming? Or do you prefer to rest by the lyche gate?"

"I'm no wilting lily, my friend. Of course I won't leave you to snoop alone."

Rose and Amaryllis walked slowly around the perimeter of St. Michael's and into the shadows of the dense cedars that gently waved in the morning breeze. All was silent except for a noisy jay in a distant corner. Rose walked ahead of Amaryllis and was standing near the one enormous monument in the churchyard.

"Amaryllis! Over here!"

Amaryllis made her way to Rose's side and gasped, "Oh, my God! Trouble Botts... sleeping on the bosom of the angel. Rose, your instincts were right!"

"I just had a feeling, Amaryllis. This is the last piece of the puzzle. Call those constables immediately! Thank God you have your phone with you. And thank God most of the Swaffham constabulary is already here. They'll have their hands full with murder and an intent to murder! Not to mention Pennington and his money-grabbing—"

"Are you sure its murder, Rose? He's in a fetal position, peaceful, as if dreaming...no punctures or other visible wounds that I can see."

"Amaryllis: look! Blood has soaked through and onto the monument beneath. I admit he's peaceful, but it cannot have been an easy ending. Horrible. To die at the hands of his one remaining relative, and with a tool he may have used every day. Brrr."

"What tool? You seem awfully sure that old Botts did him in. His own nephew? His only flesh and blood? What about Pennington? You don't think...oo, I've got to sit down a moment." Amaryllis sank down on a sturdy, square block inscribed with 'PAX'.

"While I am resting on peace, Rose, let's hear your theory on poor Trevor's demise."

"Amaryllis, Trevor was stabbed with a gimlet. Spelled G I M L E T. No, don't look: it's still there. Probably the same tool he and old Botts used to punch holes in the cedars for the insecticide they used. Then Botts just as cold heartedly used the gimlet on his own kin."

"Are you sure that Pennington wasn't in on this?"

"For your peace of mind, Amaryllis, Pennington's a crook but not a killer. If you need more proof, here is Botts' blue cap. He must have forgotten it in his rush to get away or left it deliberately. Perhaps remorse kicked in after he killed his nephew?"

"We both know that Willem Botts had practically dedicated his life to St. Michael's. We learned that the first day we walked onto the grounds. So sad."

"It *is* sad Amaryllis. He looked upon his activity in up-rooting headstones and receiving money for the lichen as a way to help Trevor get ahead in life."

"And then Trevor began to get greedy and stole pieces throughout East Plumley. Don't you think he was the thief, Rose?"

"Absolutely, dear. And then I imagine he worried old Willem about procuring more headstones. That was it for the old man. A harmless but profitable scheme quickly got out of hand. And perhaps Willem began to realize how wrong this whole affair was going."

"Oh Rose, do you think his conscience bothered him? A little?"

"Perhaps. He had to put an end to Trevor's role in the action so he killed him." Rose trembled as she considered Trouble's gruesome death.

"Amaryllis, a jury will probably hear 'act of mercy' from his legal counsel."

"Rose," said Amaryllis, slowly uprooting herself from her cold, hard perch, "you are very wise. I hope you'll be able to say a few words to old Willem. Murder is murder, but he has my sympathy . . . somewhat."

"How about leaning on the lyche gate while I call the constables? Then we'll return to the Arms and you must rest. Let me have your phone."

"We both need that dram of brandy, Rose."

Chapter Twenty-Seven

"Rose, you've spoiled me. Letting me have a lie-in. What a treat. But I am full of questions this morning. First, any word from the vicar?"

"The vicar and I had a long conversation an hour or so ago, Amaryllis. Of course, the first question he asked was, 'How is the lovely doctor?' After reassuring him you were still sleeping, and apparently fit as a fiddle, he told me he was with Botts and would look in on you as soon as he could slip away. The vicar sounded crestfallen, and no wonder. Botts confessed that he killed his nephew."

Amaryllis grimaced and said, "And we were both so sure that Botts' trifling nephew was the 'number one' evil doer here. Will you please tell me, Rose, how you found out Willem Botts cut the cord at St. Michael's?"

"Simple, Amaryllis. Old Botts had the only key to the downstairs storage closet."

"How on this green earth did you know *that?*"

"Remember when I helped with lunch for the OAP's? We had a nasty spill in the kitchen and Botts was dispatched to fetch the mop. I was assigned to help carry the cleaning bucket and watched as he pulled the key to the closet from a chain around his neck. He had to move that tall ladder to one side in order to retrieve the mop."

"And you figured all of this out during morning prayers?"

"Indeed! I prayed to the Almighty for swift guidance. Golly, I would say He heard me."

"And what about Rupert Pennington's role in this? Where does he fit in this nefarious scheme? I knew you were suspicious of him from that first introduction in the pub, but as to concrete evidence, is there any?"

"Pennington owns the warehouse where all of the stones and other stolen objects were kept. He no doubt can identify those who were extracting the lichen."

"Are they holding him in Swaffham also?"

"Absolutely. And he's singing like the proverbial canary. 'Doing all this in the name of science, trying to find a solution to the world's ills, etc. etc.' Pennington has wealth, and right or wrong, he's using that wealth to shield himself from the law. I had no solid evidence on him, but now he is incriminating himself and attempting to buy his way out with his money. East Plumley's town solicitor should be soliciting expert legal assistance if he expects to come out of this unscathed!"

"Too bad Botts doesn't have a bit of his wealth. I suppose a public defender will take his case. Why did he get mixed up in this, Rose? All for that nephew?"

"It is a sad situation. As I said, all Botts wanted was to help his nephew 'get ahead'. Probably have an education, buy a little piece of land. When he, old Botts, was approached by unnamed parties to collect lichen for a study, he was promised 'big money'. Easy! Where was the logical place to find lichen? His own backyard: St. Michael's churchyard. Willem was planning to give Trevor the 'big money' for his future. 'Fellow needs a hand-up' he told the vicar. Between tears of contrition."

"But the nephew was as guilty as Willem, don't you think? Didn't he carry the stones and deliver them to the lichen processors? And steal the town's other missing items?"

"Indeed. But Willem didn't see that as a crime. He contends that Trevor was helping because he, Willem, wasn't strong enough to handle the digging. Much less the weight of the stones. Willem and Trevor were delivering the stones to Pennington's warehouse. Botts denies he ever saw Pennington there, but that is highly unlikely."

"Why do you say that Rose?"

"I am convinced that that Rupert Pennington is the front man in this operation. Pennington is slick enough to know that lichen is a necessary ingredient of this invisible ink, and he put together an unscrupulous team to get at it."

"I commend you on your delicate choice of words, Rose. I would have said the only one *cunning* enough, but let's let it go."

"This case is bigger than East Plumley, Amaryllis. I am convinced that once London hears about this, some of their top investigative teams will be swarming up here."

"Two lives ruined, one death, and the village of East Plumley reeling in shock and disbelief. And all for the want of a simple element of nature that could become a specific ingredient for something horrific. Are you surprised at this, Rose?"

"Nothing surprises me anymore, Amaryllis. I'll hate to leave East Plumley. Though I will *not* let this crime disillusion me. Not about people, nor this lovely village. I've found every corner charming and I still have a few more to explore before meeting David in London. Speaking of which, Amaryllis, when *do* we leave? I need to plan the London itinerary with David. He's found some new galleries for us to visit."

"Oh, darling, I've been dreading to tell you. *I'm* not leaving! Coulton has asked me to stay on a bit and help him clear up a few matters. Pick up the pieces, one might say. Then he's promised to take me to the Lake District. Think of the lichen I'll find there. Would you mind dreadfully if I didn't return to London with you, Rose?"

"Oh, no, Amaryllis. As I said not three minutes ago, nothing surprises me anymore!"

Chapter Twenty-Eight

Virginia's weather in late April was glorious, and nowhere lovlier than at Wynfield Farms.

Rose and her new ten-week old Scottie, Islay, returning from the first of many walks of the day, met the Wynfield postman as he was preparing to leave.

"Stuffed your mailbox today, Mrs. McNess!" he called out cheerily.

"Oh good! No bills, of course."

"Nothin' but the good stuff today."

"Well, come Islay. Let's see what we've got," Rose called as the pair entered the Wynfield Farms lobby. She gathered her collection of mail, ("Mostly junk, I see!") as they made their way to her condo. Islay promptly found a patch of warm April sun, stretched out, and began snoring softly.

Rose sank into her maple rocker and began to sort through the clutch of papers resting in her lap. Quickly discarding the usual ads, including a come-on for new tires, she placed the one bill in her pocket before shuffling the remaining pieces in hopes of finding a letter or two. "Of course, no one writes anymore: it's all internet, email, cell phone, or heaven only knows what other devices are out there. Pity." She continued the shuffling.

"Whoa! A postcard from Amaryllis! Golly, this is a surprise!"

…postscript

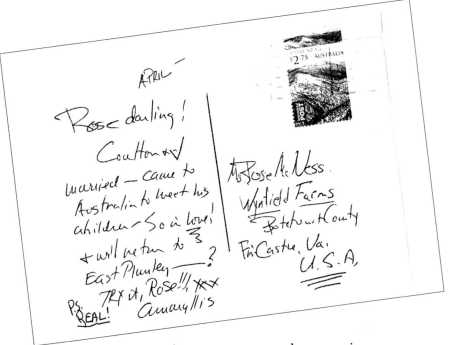

A not unexpected postscript…

Advance Praise for *ROSE IN CHARGE*

"I hear that words sprung from warmth and love, like spices from soil, or fishes from fresh waters, provide a fulfillment on a rainy day or cold evening. Books provide that extra special touch, and Barbara Dickinson has, once again, touched and embraced us with her love not only of reading but also of creating. Dickinson may entitle this charming novel *ROSE IN CHARGE*, but it is Barbara who is leading us to another wonderful vision of life. We are so lucky she shares that vision that grows from her heart's garden.

Poetically,
Nikki Giovanni"

"Barbara Dickinson's creation, Rose McNess, is a delightful wonder and she shows no signs of slowing down in her latest undercover escapade. Dickinson's sentences are a treat to savor, and the cast of characters with which she surrounds Rose is superbly drawn. Equal parts charming, smart, funny and suspenseful, this new novel is an amicable stunner."

Dr. Tom Noyes
H & SS
Penn State, Behrend
Erie, PA

Barbara Dickinson's previous novels (**A Rebellious House and Small House, Large World**) reflect both her love for the state of Virginia and her understanding of the many complexities of growing old! In this, her fourth novel, she celebrates her character's ferocity of spirit and hearty 'can-do' attitude, in everything from romance to mayhem and even, perhaps, murder.

Barbara is a graduate of Wellesley College and received a M.A.L.S. degree from Hollins University.

When not traveling, Barbara Dickinson lives in Roanoke, Virginia with her sixth Scottish terrier, *Wee Thistle of Islay*. The pair enjoys visiting local health and retirement centers where Islay works as a therapy dog. (photo courtesy Sarah Hazlegrove)